THE
HOUSE
THAT
WHISPERS

THE HOUSE THAT WHISPERS

LIN THOMPSON

LITTLE, BROWN AND COMPANY
New York Boston

Little, Brown and Company
Hachette Book Group
1290 Avenue of the Americas, New York, NY 10104
Visit us at LBYR.com

First Edition: February 2023

Little, Brown and Company is a division of Hachette Book Group, Inc. The Little, Brown name and logo are trademarks of Hachette Book Group, Inc.

The publisher is not responsible for websites (or their content) that are not owned by the publisher.

Distressed texture © Anna Timoshenko/Shutterstock.com
Scratched black background © Wilqkuku/Shutterstock.com

Little, Brown and Company books may be purchased in bulk for business, educational, or promotional use. For information, please contact your local bookseller or the Hachette Book Group Special Markets Department at special.markets@hbgusa.com.

Library of Congress Cataloging-in-Publication Data
Names: Thompson, Lin, author.
Title: The house that whispers / Lin Thompson.
Description: First edition. | New York : Little, Brown and Company, 2023. | Audience: Ages 8–12. | Summary: "Simon, an eleven-year-old coming to terms with his gender identity, is convinced that his grandmother's house is haunted." —Provided by publisher.
Identifiers: LCCN 2022031747 | ISBN 9780316277112 (hardcover) | ISBN 9780316277488 (ebook)
Subjects: CYAC: Gender identity—Fiction. | Haunted houses—Fiction. | Ghosts—Fiction. | Family life—Fiction.
Classification: LCC PZ7.1.T46795 Ho 2023 | DDC [Fic] —dc23
LC record available at https://lccn.loc.gov/2022031747

ISBNs: 978-0-316-27711-2 (hardcover), 978-0-316-27748-8 (ebook)

Printed in the United States of America

LSC-C

Printing 1, 2022

For Megan, Kate, Kevin, and Tricia

Saint Peter

SIMON IS MY SECRET NAME. I'M THE ONLY ONE WHO KNOWS IT. I picked it out during my Sunday school class last year, when Mrs. Evans was teaching us about the apostle Peter.

Me and my sisters, Talia and Rose, have to go to Sunday school every single week. Technically it's called CCD, not Sunday school, but it feels like school and it happens on Sundays, and I don't know what CCD stands for, anyway. Nanaleen just calls it our "religious education." Mom says that all of us kids can choose whatever religion or non-religion feels best for us as we get older. But everybody in her whole family is Catholic, and she wants us to know the basics.

The week I picked my name, Mrs. Evans was telling us about how the apostle Peter had been named Simon at first. She was telling us that Jesus changed his name when he picked Peter to be the first pope.

"What if Peter didn't want to change his name?" I'd asked.

Mrs. Evans sighed at me. She taught Sunday school for all the fourth and fifth graders, and she had to sigh at me a lot back when I was in elementary school. "Let's all remember to raise our hands, please."

I shot my hand up into the air and wiggled my eyebrows at her till she called on me. "What if Peter didn't want to change it?" I asked again.

"He was probably honored," Mrs. Evans told us. "Peter means 'rock.' When Jesus gave Peter his new name, he said, *Upon this rock I will build my church.*"

That didn't really answer my question, and I still didn't see why Jesus should get to walk around telling people what their names had to be. Besides, I liked the name Simon a lot better than Peter.

So I took it. It's not like St. Peter needs it anymore.

After class that day, I looked up the meaning of the name Simon, too. It turns out that Simon means "listen."

I've never been a good listener. Dad says I have selective hearing, because sometimes when he tells me to empty the dishwasher, if I'm busy with homework or practicing my soccer knee bounces, I don't hear him. And Mom says I jump to conclusions instead of listening. She says I sometimes make up the answer I want to hear instead of listening to find out what the answer actually is.

But maybe Peter wasn't really a rock, solid and steady and firm, until Jesus named him after one. Maybe a name can be something you *want* to be. Something you work to become. Like if I call myself Simon, then maybe, slowly, I'll turn into a better listener.

And, you know, a boy. The kind of boy that other people can see and recognize, instead of me being the only one who knows it.

I *want* the name to fit me.

I don't know what Mrs. Evans would say if she knew about my secret name. But probably she'd tell me that if my name's Simon, I should be doing a better job listening in class.

LOOKOUT

MY OLDER SISTER TALIA TURNED THIRTEEN THIS YEAR, WHICH means that now, whenever we're driving someplace with only one of our parents, she gets to ride in the front seat. It's something that's come up a lot more over the past couple of months. Whenever we're riding with Mom *and* Dad, Dad usually drives, and Mom sits up front, and then Talia, Rose, and I cram shoulder to shoulder in the back seat like sardines. It's awkward and annoying, and I always used to complain about it.

Now, though, whenever the back holds just Rose and me, the car feels a little empty. Like it's too big for our family.

For the trip to Nanaleen's house, Dad is driving, and Talia's riding up front.

"You're kicking my seat," Talia tells me, frowning back at me over her headrest.

"Oh, sorry," I say. I make my feet stop moving. I hadn't realized I was kicking.

Talia sighs. "It's fine. I know how you are on long car rides."

She means that on long trips, I get so bored and fidgety I about crawl out of my own skin. We've been stuck in the car for over two hours now, which in my opinion is two hours too many.

"Now you're tapping your fingers," Rose complains from the other side of the back seat.

I clench up my hands to stop, but that just makes my fingers want to move even more. I stuff my fists under my legs. Dad's leaning forward against the steering wheel with his shoulders rigid, squinting along the foggy road up ahead. It's Sunday afternoon. Usually when we visit Nanaleen's, the fog would've melted away by this time of the day. Summer afternoons in Kentucky are too hot for fog. But it's October now, not summer, and this isn't our usual visit to Nanaleen's.

"Cool it, Bradleys," Dad says without taking his eyes off the road. Sometimes, when he's stressed out, he calls us all by our last name like he's a cranky camp counselor. "If y'all are bored, you can help me watch for deer."

It's not the right time for deer to be out, probably, but the fog makes Dad worried. If an animal runs out in front of the car, he'll barely see it coming. Then again, it's probably not the fog's fault that Dad's worried. He's probably just worried because he's always worried.

"Sorry," I say again.

I really am. Right before we'd left home, Mom had told me, "Don't make trouble for your dad, okay? He's stressed." I stick my face against the window for deer lookout duty.

In the front seat, Talia's turned back to her phone already. She's barely looked up from it this whole drive. She's been texting somebody, but I can't see who. Talia just says, "Mmm," not even paying attention to me anymore.

I let my forehead rest against the glass so that

every bump in the road makes my teeth rattle against each other. No deer. There's so much fog that everything outside the car looks blurry and white. Twenty feet around us in any direction, the world dissolves—there's trees, and there's trees, and then there's just nothing.

Nanaleen's house is deep in the woods. It's a mile outside the closest town, five miles from the closest Walmart, and a hundred fifty miles from our house back in Louisville. I feel my legs starting to swing on their own, and I have to stop my foot just before it kicks the front seat again—the seat where Mom should be sitting.

We're almost a hundred fifty miles from where we left Mom.

Ghost Town

OUR GRANDMOTHER NANALEEN LIVES IN THE OLD FAMILY HOME outside Misty Valley. The town isn't far enough east to be in the actual Appalachian Mountains, but it still has some impressive hills. Nanaleen says the town got its name because of the fog. When the mist rolls in from the actual mountains, it gets penned into the valley by the hills on all sides and covers up the whole town in a cloudy blanket.

During the summer, the fog usually clears out before the sun's even finished rising. Misty Valley is always busy in the summertime. That's when we usually come to stay with Nanaleen—the whole month of July, every summer of my life. The town is right beside a lake, and as soon as the weather starts warming up, it gets flooded with families coming to camp or hike or fish or swim. They rent out the fancy vacation cottages down by the lakeshore, and there are kids on the beach from sunup to sundown. The shops on Main Street are always packed.

As our car pulls onto Main Street now, I keep expecting the fog to disappear and the street to fill up, but it doesn't. Most of the shops are closed for the off-season. Beyond the empty buildings, I catch a glimpse of the Scooper Dooper, which is the little blue ice cream shack down by the boat ramp that we always ride our bikes to. On nice days, you usually have to wait in line for twenty or thirty minutes just to get a cone. But now the Scooper Dooper is boarded up and empty.

Frazer's Market is still open, though, which is good, because Dad has to stop for gas. Frazer's is the only gas station in town, right in the middle of Main Street. There are days when it's nearly impossible to get a pump, but today we're the only car in sight. Dad eyes the price on the sign, frowning.

"Twenty cents more than it was in Campbells-ville," he mutters as he digs out his wallet.

"Can we go say hi to Mr. Ben?" I ask. Mr. Ben is the owner of Frazer's. I'm trying to wave at him through the front window of the store, but I don't think he's seen me yet.

"Not today. I'm sure you all will come visit him this week."

"Can I go use the bathroom?" Rose asks.

"No." Dad swings himself out of the car, but then he seems to think again, and he ducks back in through the opening. "We're two minutes away from Nana-leen's," he tells Rose. "Just...everybody stay put."

He closes the car door harder than he has to behind him. He's got his phone out now, and he's tapping something out on the calculator. With the engine off, the car is clicking a little as it cools down.

Don't make trouble for your dad, okay? I wait till I'm sure Dad can't hear us before I say, "Why can't we get out?"

Talia swivels around to look at me over her

headrest again. "Because if you go inside, you're going to ask to get snacks."

"No, I won't," I say, even though I was definitely going to ask to get snacks.

"And Dad doesn't want to have to say no."

I shrug. "Well, then, he could say yes."

"Just wait and eat something at Nanaleen's," Talia says, frowning back down at her phone. "He's already having to pay for gas."

Dad's still calculating something, and I realize he's figuring out how much gas he'll need to drive back to Louisville. Getting gas didn't used to involve math—Mom and Dad would just keep pumping it till the tank was full.

I lean my face against the window again and peer down Main Street. With the shops all closed up, with the fog everywhere, it feels like the end of the world. It feels like we're the only people left alive.

Mom has always said that Misty Valley becomes a ghost town from September until May, but I never really believed her. When I was little, I thought she meant it literally. I thought ghosts and spirits would start roaming around town every fall. Now I know she just meant that most people leave. Only the permanent residents stick around, like Nanaleen now, and like Mom and her sisters when they were growing up here.

For the other three-quarters of the year, the town feels lonely and empty. Like it's full of holes.

The Old O'Hagan House

DAD PUTS EXACTLY TEN DOLLARS OF GAS IN THE CAR BEFORE we set off down the highway toward Nanaleen's house. He turns into Nanaleen's long driveway and starts inching up the gravel at a snail's pace. I'm about ready to explode from being stuck in the car, and Rose has her legs crossed tight in a way that means her question back at Frazer's wasn't just an excuse to go inside—she really does have to use the bathroom. Dad flicks the brights on to cut through the fog. They hit the old house at the top of the driveway like a spotlight.

Nanaleen's is the oldest house I've ever been inside. It's a big two-story farmhouse with a wraparound porch and a rough stone chimney attached to the front, poking up over the roof like a tower. The outer siding is faded, and the paint on the window frames and porch columns has started peeling off. But you can still sense that the house was impressive back in the day.

All the year-rounders in Misty Valley call it the old O'Hagan house, even though none of us has the last name O'Hagan anymore. But our great-great-grandfather did, and he was the one who built it.

Dad parks beside the front porch, and I've started unbuckling before he even turns the car off.

"Scoot, scoot, scoot," I tell Rose, because the door on my side of the car always gets stuck. Dad tried to fix the latch himself, but when that didn't work, he told us to just live with it and use the other side to get in and out. Rose opens her door, too slow, and slides out of the car, also too slow. Finally I can clamber past her and flop down on the driveway outside.

"At last," I say, pretending to kiss the gravel, like I've washed up on a desert island after months at sea. *"At last."*

Talia comes around the front of the car and peers down at me. "You're so dramatic," she says, but she has to try hard not to smile.

"Bathroom," Rose says. She takes off running for the house.

"I'm not bringing in your bag!" Talia yells after her, along with a name I'm not allowed to say.

"Talia," Dad says. "Cool it."

"What?" Talia says innocently. She pops open the trunk and drags her duffel bag out of it with one hand, and then she uses the other to pick up her winter jacket, which Mom made her bring. "I don't have any extra hands," she explains.

Dad sighs. "Simon, can you take Rose's bag?"

He doesn't say "Simon," of course. He doesn't know my secret name. Nobody except me does. But I change his words in my head, and then I say, "On it," and hop up to grab Rose's suitcase out of the back.

By the time I've dug out my own backpack and slung it over my arm, the house's front door is wide open, and there in the doorway is Nanaleen.

"You made it!" she says. Rose gives her the quickest hug in history before rushing inside for the toilet. Nanaleen waits there on the porch for the rest of us, her pink, veiny hands propped on her hips as she watches us unload. "How was the drive?"

"Not bad," Dad says. I'm pretty sure even if we'd gotten into a five-car pileup, he'd answer that question in the same way. Dad's a worrier, but he never wants anyone *else* to worry.

"Good, good," Nanaleen says.

Nanaleen is Mom's mother, our grandma. Her real name is Rosaleen, but when Talia was little, she got confused about why she was supposed to call her Nana when grown-ups would sometimes call her Rosaleen instead. So Talia combined them. We've all been calling her Nanaleen for longer than I've been alive.

I tuck Rose's suitcase under one arm and pull my backpack onto the other. Then, for good measure, I grab Rose's pillow and my pillow and my extra pair of sneakers that I couldn't fit into my backpack, and I stagger up toward the house.

"You grew," Nanaleen tells me, beaming, when I get to the front porch. She wraps me and all my bags up into a hug. Nanaleen gives the best hugs. Her skin's pale and soft and feels like well-used tissue paper. She's old, obviously, but she's never *seemed* old. She's always excited and full of energy and wants to do eighteen different things at once. Mom says I'm just like her in that way.

"You just saw me in July," I remind her.

"That just makes it more impressive. And your haircut! It suits you." She gives my hair a ruffle, even though she's already seen the pictures.

"Thanks." I can feel myself grinning. Mom let me cut it short at the start of this school year—she probably would've let me longer ago, but that was when I finally asked. Mom calls it a "pixie cut." I think that's just what people call short hair when it's on someone they think is a girl.

"And here's Talia!" Nanaleen hugs Talia next, and Talia lets her, even though Talia would probably bite almost anyone else who tried that.

Dad's hauling everything else from the car up

the porch steps, panting a little. He always likes to carry everything inside in one trip. He says he likes the challenge of it.

Nanaleen peeks over his shoulder at our now empty car. "Where's Tessa?" she asks.

Tessa is our mom. Just like that, as soon as Nanaleen asks that question, this cold feeling starts in my throat. It pours down through my chest and into my arms and legs, flowing too fast to stop, like the water from the garden spigot when you turn it all the way up. I swallow hard to try to push it back.

Dad's blinking at Nanaleen. "She stayed back at the house, remember?" he says. "I'm driving back tonight. It's just the kids this visit."

Nanaleen's smile slips as she blinks right back at him, confused. Her skin looks more papery than it did when we were here in July—more transparent.

"Oh," she says. Then she smiles again and her face smooths back out. So fast I think I imagined it. I tell myself that I probably *did* imagine it. "Oh, right. Of course."

"Take your stuff upstairs, okay?" Dad tells Talia and me.

I don't need telling twice. I swallow again and then one more time until I can push the cold feeling out of my body. I pull out a smile. "Sure," I say, and I squeeze past Nanaleen toward the door.

But Talia hasn't moved. She's still on the porch, frowning at Dad and Nanaleen.

"Talia," Dad says. "Go get unpacked."

Talia makes a huffing sound, but then she follows me inside. "*I* know when I'm being dismissed," she mutters. Whatever that means.

When we visit Nanaleen over the summer, Mom always comes with us for the whole month. But this trip, everything's turned crooked, like I'm looking at it all sideways. It's fall break instead of July. Talia, Rose, and I are staying here, and Mom and Dad aren't. They're both spending the week back in Louisville and then coming back to pick us up next weekend. Dad keeps saying they need a "reset." Mom says they "need time to talk." I guess they can't reset or talk to each other when we're around.

I think about the extra seat in the car on the drive here—the empty space between me and Rose in the back because Talia was riding up front in what should've been Mom's seat. The car without Mom feels too big and empty and lonely, like Misty Valley in the off-season. We've got holes of our own. A ghost family.

Smelly Towels

AS SOON AS I'M INSIDE THE HOUSE, I CATCH THE SMELL.

Nanaleen's house always has a specific smell: musty and old, but not in a bad way. Usually it smells like when Mom used to take us with her to the huge university library and I'd find the oldest book I could and stick my nose inside the pages. Dusty and almost a little sweet. I always notice it when we first come to visit, even though once we've been inside for a couple hours, it kind of fades.

But the smell that hits me this time is different. It's musty and old, and definitely in a bad way. It's sour. Like an old washcloth. It smells like Nanaleen's dragged her whole linen closet of towels through the mud and then left them in a pile on the stairs to dry. Which Nanaleen would never, ever do.

It's just one more thing that's a little bit wrong.

Talia and I haul our bags upstairs. Nanaleen's house has a main floor, an upstairs, and an attic. Whenever we visit, me, Talia, and Rose always share the attic bedroom. It's the same bedroom Mom and Aunt Bridget and Aunt Shannon shared when they were growing up here, and then before them, Nanaleen and her sisters, Margie and Brie. Mom sometimes calls it the Sisters' Dormitory since it's had all of these generations of sisters sleeping in it. But thinking of me, Talia, and Rose as "sisters" doesn't really fit anymore, so now I just call it the Dormitory.

The door to the attic staircase always gets warped and sticks in its frame, but Talia gives it a couple tugs till it pulls open. We have to climb the narrow stairs one at a time, our bags bumping against the walls the whole way up.

The Dormitory stretches the whole length of

the house. The ceiling is low and sloped, all yellow-white drywall that's starting to sag in some places and crack in others. I dump Rose's suitcase on her bed at the top of the stairs, and then I haul my stuff over to my own bed at the far end of the room. I stick up my hand as I walk, just like I always do in here, and try to touch the ceiling at its highest spot, where it comes to a point in the middle. Even when I'm on my tiptoes, my fingers can't quite skim it.

I'll probably be tall enough to touch it by our visit next summer. According to Dad, I'm growing like a weed.

My bed's just the same as always: same blue-and-purple quilt, same tucked-in sheets, same brownish water stain running along the sloped ceiling just above it. But when I plop myself down, the mattress creaks more than I remember.

Talia throws her bag down on her own bed so hard it bounces. "Home sweet home, I guess," she says.

"What're you so cranky about?" I say.

"She's always cranky," Rose says, and just like

that she pops up the stairs, back from the bath-room. She ignores Talia's glare and starts unload-ing things from her bag into a tidy pile on the floor: her notebook, her pencils, a stack of library books about chemistry. Just about every month, Rose changes her mind about what she wants to do when she grows up. Right now, she's decided to become a scientist. "Mom says it's *puberty*."

"It is not." Talia sniffs.

Rose shrugs. "Whatever you say."

It's still light outside, but in the Dormitory, you can barely tell. The window between Talia's and my beds at the front of the house is always a little grimy, no matter how many times Nanaleen Win-dexes it. One of the bulbs in the overhead light is burned out, and the two that are still working flicker for a second. Right after, I hear the furnace all the way down in the basement kicking on. Old electrical system, I guess.

But I can't help thinking about the summer that Talia, Rose, and me spent our vacation here hunt-ing for ghosts. That was years ago—before I was

Simon, before I'd pieced together that *sister* wasn't quite the right word for me. When Talia had first made up the game, when she'd suggested we look for ghosts, we all thought it was pretend. Maybe Talia and Rose still do.

But sometimes I wonder.

That cold feeling that had poured through me on the porch is back now, inching up my spine. Ready to take back over me if I let it. I push it back down where it belongs.

"Do you guys want to see if Nanaleen made snickerdoodles?" I ask.

Nanaleen loves baking, and every time we visit, she fills up the kitchen with homemade snacks. Her snickerdoodles are legendary: crisp on the outside and soft on the inside, and always rolled in so much cinnamon sugar that they can make you sneeze.

Rose and Talia both grumble okay and we go down to the kitchen, where Nanaleen brings out the cookie tin and lets us stuff our faces even though we haven't had supper yet.

So at least some things are the same.

✳✳✳

Dad drives back to Louisville that night, right after we eat supper. He reminds us all about fifty times to be good for Nanaleen this week.

"Behave yourselves, Bradleys," he says, with this frown like he's trying his best to be stern. Then he plops a kiss on each of our foreheads. "We'll call every day, okay? Mom will want to talk to you, too. And we're both gonna drive down to pick you up again on Saturday, okay?"

Whenever he starts saying "okay" like that, I know he's worrying again. I make myself smile big so he knows we're all right. "See you on Saturday," I tell him.

After he's gone, though, as Nanaleen lets us all three stay up late playing Parcheesi and then as we're getting ready for bed, I just keep picturing him and Mom back at home, alone. Rattling around a house that's too big for them without Talia, Rose, and me to help fill it.

I keep waiting for my nose to get used to the

house's musty smell, just like it usually does. But even when I wake up hours later that night, I still notice the smell. The Dormitory is pitch-black, and the sloped ceiling above my bed is sloping lower than feels right, and the room is colder than it's supposed to be. Colder than it is in summer, anyway.

And everything still smells like old, rotten towels.

Secret Name

MOM ALWAYS TELLS ME I HAVE A VERY ACTIVE IMAGINATION.
She says I imagine things so hard, I make them
true in my mind. Sometimes she's right. When
we were little, Talia and I used to pretend we had
superpowers—she always had super strength,
and I had super speed. I *knew* we were just playing
around. I *knew* it was just a game. But sometimes,
when I'd start running, I could almost feel my hero
powers kick in, and suddenly I'd be going faster
than fast. In my brain, I'd be totally convinced I
was running faster than anybody ever had.

And sometimes I make up memories instead—
my brain can trick itself into remembering stuff I

wasn't alive for, or stuff that never even happened. Nanaleen will tell a family story, and I'll remember being there for it, only to learn the story took place before I was even born. Or I'll have a dream, and the next morning, I'll be so sure that the stuff that happened in it was real.

But I think sometimes it goes the other way, too. Sometimes, things are just true, even though I don't realize they're true at the beginning. Sometimes I have to start out believing something is imaginary until I'm finally ready to understand that it's real.

Simon started out like that.

When I started using my secret name, I told myself that it was just part of a game. Like playing pretend in my own head. I would decide, *I'm a boy and my name is Simon*, and then suddenly every single thing I did turned new and exciting. A teacher would call on me with my old name, and I'd think, *Actually, my name is Simon*, and this warm feeling would start in my chest, like I was carrying around a little glowing light. Or I'd be washing dishes with Dad and out of nowhere I'd remember, *I'm Simon*, and I'd find myself smiling till my face hurt.

Sometimes I write my full name on scraps of paper just to see it outside my own head: *Simon Bradley, Simon Bradley*, over and over again. Then I wad the paper up and tuck it at the bottom of the trash can in the bathroom so nobody will notice it or pull it out.

I don't remember when I first realized I wasn't a girl. Maybe I always kind of knew that part. The bigger thing was realizing that everyone else *thought* I was a girl.

But earlier this year, one of Mom's friends came out as transgender. When she changed her name and started having people use *she* and *her* pronouns when they talked about her, Mom sat the three of us kids down and explained what that meant. She wanted us to understand so we could be supportive. I usually only take out comics from the library when my class goes every week during school, but I started checking out more and more books about trans people and reading things online. There was so much to learn. So many different words and labels for people's experiences.

I don't know exactly what gender label fits me best. Maybe I'm a trans boy. Maybe I'm nonbinary and don't really fit into the categories of "boy" or "girl." Maybe I'm both, or no gender at all.

The thing I do know is that I like being Simon. Even if I thought at first that I was just playing pretend, that was never really the whole truth. Because the game never really ended.

By now I just let myself be Simon all the time. Thinking of myself as Simon makes my whole body feel different. It lets my spine relax and my lungs work a little better. It lets me stand up taller and uncurl my shoulders. When I remember I'm Simon, I get so happy sometimes—that overflowing kind of happy that courses through me, warm and glowing, all the way to my fingertips. It makes my chest ache, but in a good way—like I can't hold it all inside me. Like I'm trying to hold on to the sun.

I haven't gotten that too-big happy feeling from

many other things. Maybe when I've scored a goal for my soccer team, or when I wake up on Christmas morning, or when I'm eating Nanaleen's snickerdoodles. But with my secret name, I don't have to wait for some special occasion. I can just remember that I'm Simon and feel that glow start in my chest. Every time it happens, it's like remembering: *Oh. Right. This is what happy feels like.*

I haven't told anyone else about my secret name, though. It feels so new, like a baby bird that's not ready to fly out of the nest yet. When people around me use my old name, I fix it in my head. When they talk about me with the wrong pronouns, I change them—usually to *he* or *him*, but I'm learning other sets of pronouns that I could try out, too.

If I told the rest of my family about being Simon, I think they'd be supportive. But I don't think I'm ready for things to change. There's an awful lot of things changing already.

And if I'm totally honest, maybe I don't want the changes to be my fault.

INSIDE JOBS AND OUTSIDE JOBS

I WAKE UP EARLY ON MONDAY MORNING SO I CAN HELP NANALEEN bake cinnamon rolls.

In Nanaleen's house, baking is an inside job, which means it's a "girl job." It's one of the skills she teaches me and Rose and Talia and our cousin Kennedy. Meanwhile, Kennedy's brothers, Ethan and Owen, learn how to help with all the outside chores. Those are the "boy jobs."

It's sexist and silly, and we all know it. I think even Nanaleen knows it. Mom says it's a holdover from how Nanaleen was raised. Nanaleen had two sisters and three brothers, and when they were growing up, the boys always had to do the outside work: growing the vegetables, splitting firewood, fixing anything that broke on the house or the car. The girls did the inside work: cooking, cleaning, washing clothes in the big sink in the basement. When Mom and Aunt Shannon and Aunt Bridget were kids, Nanaleen had all three of them do the inside work, even though they didn't have any brothers and so Papaw had to do all the outside work mostly by himself.

Papaw died before I was born, and so Nanaleen's been doing the inside *and* outside work herself for my whole life. But she still separates it out for us grandkids—most of the time, at least. There are exceptions. Talia got really interested in gardening for a while, and so Nanaleen taught her how to water and weed the vegetable beds. And sometimes Ethan and Owen get her to let them run her giant vacuum cleaner that sounds like an angry bear.

It's not that Nanaleen is so strict about who can do what chores anymore. It's just that, unless you ask for something different, you'll get dropped into the jobs for whatever gender everybody assumes you are.

I don't like that baking is one of her "girl jobs." But I still like baking.

Sometimes Nanaleen gets the canisters of pre-made cinnamon rolls from the grocery store, but this morning, we're making them from scratch. That means we're using real yeast from the little jar in the back of the fridge, and we're stirring in flour and sugar and water and milk. Nanaleen splits the mixture into two portions so she and I can both knead it into dough side by side on the kitchen table.

Nanaleen has a big mixer on her counter that can knead the dough for you—Mom and the aunts all pooled their money and gave it to her for Christmas a couple years ago. But she almost never uses it, and she definitely never uses it for cinnamon rolls.

"You have to *feel* the dough," she tells me as we knead, which is what she says every time.

"I'm feeling it," I say. I hold up my hands to show her: There's wet flour stuck all over my palms, and my fingers are glued together. My dough isn't really dough yet. It's a sticky mess. "Is it supposed to be feeling me right back?"

"Keep kneading it. It'll smooth out."

Rose started out helping us make the rolls this morning, but she doesn't like her hands getting messy, so she left partway through. I thought about telling her that if she wants to be a scientist, she's probably going to have to get used to mess. But I didn't want her to change her mind. I like baking best when it's just me and Nanaleen.

"How's everything at home?" Nanaleen asks as we work. She says it carefully, like maybe she's actually trying to ask something else.

"Okay, I guess," I say. "You know. Pretty normal."

"You doing...okay?" The way she pauses before she gets to "okay" tells me she's *definitely* trying to ask something else. "I've been worrying about you three. I know it must be tough with—"

"I'm great." As soon as I say it, I feel bad for cutting Nanaleen off—but not bad enough to go back. I smash the dough against the table a little harder than I mean to, trying to figure out how to convince her that she shouldn't worry about us. "I mean, I've mostly just been busy. With school and stuff."

I guess she gets the message that I don't want to talk about home, because she lets it go. "How're you liking your new school?" she asks instead.

"It's all right."

"What's that word your mom uses? STEP, or STAMP?"

"You mean STEM?" I ask. "A STEM academy. But that's not me, that's Talia."

Talia goes to a special all-girls magnet school that's focused on science and math. I could've maybe started there this year, too, but when my whole grade took the admission exam last spring, I bombed the math section. Kind of on purpose. Mom and Dad had started talking about middle schools and asking if I wanted to follow Talia, and I just kept picturing myself stuck at an all-girls school. I kind of panicked.

"My school's fine, though," I say now. "We get to do art a lot. And everybody's nice."

"Good. Thank goodness. You hear sometimes about how *rude* folks can be in the city."

Nanaleen always calls Louisville "the city," like it's New York City or something. I guess compared to Misty Valley, it basically is.

"Are you making new friends?" she asks.

I scrunch up my nose. "Nanale-e-e-en," I say, because that's how Talia would answer, because it's easier to pretend the embarrassing thing is the question itself and not the fact that I *haven't* really been making new friends.

"What?" Nanaleen says, putting her floury hands on her hips, but she looks like she's holding back a smile. "I'm not allowed to ask you kids about your social lives?"

"Yes, okay?" I say, laughing. "I'm making friends!"

It's not totally a lie. There are people I'm friend*ly* with. There are people I eat lunch with and people I talk to before class, and last month I even went to a sleepover at Amina Kaur's house. But I've never really had a best friend, or friends I want to hang out with outside of school. I've always just had siblings.

That was always enough.

Nanaleen flicks flour at me, and then she checks

my dough and adjusts my hands so I'm working with the heel of my palm instead of my fingers. Now that we've been kneading for a while, it's all mixing together, just like Nanaleen said it would. Now it's all just dough, smooth and stretchy, and if you didn't know, if you hadn't watched when we were measuring out ingredients, you probably couldn't pick out all the things that had gone into it. It feels a little bit like magic. Rose would probably point out that it's just science.

"Had any soccer games yet this year?" Nanaleen asks.

This heavy feeling starts making its way through my chest, like the gravity around me suddenly got turned up. I keep my eyes focused on my dough. "Nah, I'm not doing soccer anymore," I say like it's no big deal.

"What? Why not?"

"Just wasn't really into it." Then I change the subject before she can ask any more questions.

The truth is that my old soccer league started splitting the sixth graders into boys and girls, and

I didn't want to play on the girls' team. Which is a bummer, because soccer was something I'm actually good at.

I keep kneading my dough ball against the table for a while longer, just the way Nanaleen's shown me. Squish it down hard with the heels of my hands, and then turn it, and then squish it down again. Squish, turn, repeat. When my arms are starting to wear out, Nanaleen holds my dough up in front of the ceiling light and stretches out a little section of it till it's thin enough to almost see through. The light glows through it from the other side.

"And there we go!" Nanaleen says. She pats my cheek with her floury hand. She sounds totally thrilled, like she hasn't done this whole process a gazillion times before. Maybe she gets the magic of it just like I do. "It passes the windowpane test."

"A-plus," I say.

She tugs the old recipe card toward her to check the next step. Whenever Mom or Dad cooks, they'll usually pull the recipe up on their phone, but Nanaleen's recipes are always handwritten on little index cards, or cut out from the newspaper a thousand years ago, or torn off the back of a cereal box. She keeps them all in a folder in the cabinet over the fridge.

"A teaspoon of salt," she reads, reaching for the saltshaker.

"We already did that one," I tell her.

"Right. I was just testing you." She moves her finger down the list. It's written out in Nanaleen's cramped, slanting cursive. "Mm...half a cup of whole milk."

"We already did that, too."

For a second, her smile slips again, just like it did yesterday on the porch with Dad. It's more obvious now—either because the moment of her missing smile lasts longer, or just because I'm watching her closer than I had been.

All of a sudden I've got this bad, bad feeling—I can't figure out how else to describe it. It's shaky and sharp and just...bad. I'm suddenly afraid that Nanaleen is going to keep guessing at the recipe's next step and keep getting it wrong. I jump in before she can take another shot.

"We make the cinnamon filling next," I tell her. "While the dough rests."

"Right," Nanaleen says. "I don't know where my brain's at." Her smile has smoothed back out. I don't even see the moment when it happens—I just see that it has. I push the bad feeling back down, just like that.

We mix together the cinnamon and sugar that'll go inside the rolls. Nanaleen sends me to the fridge for butter, and we melt a wedge of it in the blue ceramic bowl with a chip on one side, the same bowl Nanaleen's used for microwaving butter for as long as I can remember. None of that takes very long, though, and soon we're twiddling our thumbs and watching the clock. The dough is supposed to rest for fifteen minutes, according to Nanaleen's card.

"Can't we just start rolling it out?" I ask. "It's close."

"Patience," Nanaleen says. I make a stink face at that, and Nanaleen laughs. "Maybe that's our sign that it's time for a break."

PICTURE-PERFECT

BREAK TIME WITH NANALEEN MEANS SITTING IN THE LIVING room and drinking black tea. Well, Nanaleen drinks tea. She settles into her recliner and sips it slow and relaxed, just like always, like it's the best drink in the entire world.

I know for a fact that's not true. She let me try her tea once. It tasted like hot water and dirt.

I pour myself some orange juice from the fridge instead and follow her into the living room. Rose is watching the Discovery Channel on Nanaleen's TV, but she pauses it when we come in. The screen is frozen on a family of deer with their little white tails standing up, getting ready to run away from something.

"Is it time to eat yet?" Rose asks.

"Not yet," I say. "We're taking a break while the dough rests. Where's Talia?"

Rose shrugs. "Last I saw, she was being boring upstairs."

"Being boring" means that Talia was on her phone. She's been glued to it lately—even at Nanaleen's, even though the cell phone signal out here is pretty bad. Nanaleen still keeps a landline hooked up and mostly just uses that, and Rose and I don't have phones yet, even though Talia got hers when she was my age. Mom says I have to show I can be responsible first. (She made that rule last year after I forgot my water bottle and sneakers at soccer practice for the third time in a row.)

"She'll come down when she smells the cinnamon rolls," Nanaleen assures us.

Rose starts telling Nanaleen about the deer on the show she'd been watching, and Nanaleen blinks her eyes wide and asks lots of questions like she's proving that she's paying attention. I don't bother. With all of Nanaleen's questions for me about home and school, I feel like I've been playing dodgeball with all the things I don't want to talk about. So now, I let myself stop listening.

Instead I start doing my usual study of the photos in frames hanging on the wall above the couch. I've seen them all before, but I like looking at them every time. I like imagining what's happening in each one and committing all the faces to memory.

Nanaleen's house is full of old family photos—they cover not only this wall but also the front hallway and the dining room and the landing upstairs. And she's got a whole spare bedroom that she calls the "history room" because she keeps shelves and shelves of old albums of even more photos in there, all arranged by year.

Not all the photos are old, of course—the albums go as recently as last year, and Nanaleen has enough frames to show off photos from every generation. The front hallway has most of the newer ones: lots of pictures of me and Talia and Rose, and pictures of our cousins, and pictures from Nanaleen's big seventieth birthday bash last summer that Mom took on her phone and got printed at Walmart. The upstairs hallway has ones of Mom and her sisters as kids, all of them with goofy clothes and haircuts. And in the dining room, Nanaleen's hung up ones of her and her siblings as adults. Those photos are grainy and faded, like all the colors got wrung out in the wash.

The photos over the couch, though, are so old that they don't have any color at all. These are the photos from when Nanaleen was a little kid.

I like these the best. Something about black-and-white photos makes everything in them seem like a story. Like an old book you've read a thousand times where you always know what's going to happen next. Maybe I only think that because I've looked at *these* photos a thousand times. Because I've already imagined what's happening in each one. Every person in them is familiar, even though nearly all of them are dead by now.

There's one of Nanaleen's three brothers up in the big oak tree out back, all of them hanging off different branches like monkeys. They're grinning straight at you, and I like to imagine their mom telling them to hold that pose while she runs to set up the camera.

There's one of Nanaleen and her sister Margie with their arms slung around each other's shoulders, caught mid-laugh. That one, I've decided, was supposed to be posed, but then Nanaleen told a joke at the last second and they both busted up.

There's a bunch of photos of Nanaleen's mom and dad and all six kids. They're from different years—you can tell because you can see the kids getting older in each one. In most of them, the whole family is lined up and smiling in front of the same house Nanaleen still lives in now.

In all these black-and-white photos, everyone looks so happy. A perfect family. I've seen plenty of pictures of Mom, Dad, Talia, Rose, and me just like this.

We're all pretty good at *looking* happy.

I'm skimming through the photos of Nanaleen and her whole family in front of the house when my eyes get caught on one.

Nanaleen and her siblings are older in this photo than they are in most of the others here. It must be one of the last on this wall. There's only five of the kids in it, though—Nanaleen's oldest sister, Brianna, is missing. When I've seen this photo before, I've just kind of assumed that she was the one behind the camera, taking the picture. But suddenly I don't know if that's true. I don't think I've ever asked.

"Where's Brianna in this one?" I ask.

Too late, I realize I cut into Rose's explanation about the TV deer. She frowns at me with this little line creasing her forehead. Sometimes, when Rose frowns, she stops looking like an eight-year-old and starts looking exactly like Dad does when he's trying to be stern.

"Sorry," I say. "I'll—" I clamp my mouth shut and mime locking it.

Rose sighs. "It's okay."

"Nanaleen?" I ask, and Nanaleen leans forward in her recliner to see which photo I'm pointing at.

"That was probably after Brie moved out," Nanaleen says.

"Where'd she move out to?" I ask. "Did she go to college or something?"

"Mm," Nanaleen says as she takes a long sip of her tea, and then she shakes her head. "She just moved out. Settled down in California, I think."

"You *think*?" I say. As soon as the words are out of my mouth I realize how rude it sounds. But I'm trying to wrap my mind around having your sister leave home and not being absolutely, one-hundred-percent positive about where she's gone to.

"How old was she?" Rose asks.

Nanaleen thinks for a long moment. "Seventeen, I guess? I was ten, and she was seven years older than me."

Seventeen. That's only four years older than Talia is now. I try to imagine if Talia left home and moved across the country. That bad feeling has started creeping over me again, and I have to make my whole back go stiff to stop myself from shivering. Rose is asking Nanaleen about a different photo on the wall, so I don't think either of them notices me tensing up, at least. Still, I feel rattled.

I find the last family photo that *does* have Brie in it. Based on the ages the other kids are between the two photos, I'd guess this one was taken a couple years before the one where she's missing. All the kids are wearing matching overalls here. Brie stands with her hand on Nanaleen's shoulder, and they're both beaming.

Nanaleen looks like Rose, I realize. Maybe it's just because she's almost the same age Rose is now, but they've got the same soft crinkle to their eyes, the same fine, fluffy hair that pokes out in different directions—although Rose's is wilder because Rose never wants to brush hers. And even though Brie is older than me in this picture, she looks a lot like me: pale face and pointed chin and ears that stick out just a little. Her smile is just a little bit mischievous, like Mom says mine always is in photos. She's even got her hair in a pixie cut— or just a short haircut, I guess.

I look back and forth between the two photos: the one with Brie and the one without her. Back and forth. Over and over. I do it enough times that my eyes get confused and start to think that the second photo, the one from after she'd moved out, *does* have her in it after all.

I blink.

No, of course not. It's just the five other kids lined up, and their mom and dad on either end.

I blink again, trying to figure out why I got confused. Why did I think there was an extra person in the picture?

And then—there it is again.

There are six kids.

No, not six kids, I realize—there are only five people lined up between the parents. There's Nanaleen. There's her sister Margie. There are their three brothers.

But there's something else, too.

It isn't Brie. Instead, in the same place Brie had been in the other photo, just over Nanaleen's shoulder—there's an eerie, shadowy figure. Not even a figure, really. It's more like an outline. I can't see it clearly when I look straight at it, only when I'm looking at the space around it. It pulls my eyes in. The outline is shaped almost like a person—or like the empty hole where a person should be.

Very slowly, that cold tingle starts up my spine again. This time, I don't catch it in time to stop myself from shuddering. It rattles right through me. On the other side of the shudder, the cold still has me in it, and I shudder again without being able to stop. It's like my body is trying to shake the bad feeling off—and it's not working.

Dread, my brain says suddenly, crystal clear. That's the feeling I was trying to describe earlier. It's dread.

"You cold?"

It's Nanaleen asking—Nanaleen now, instead of kid Nanaleen in the photo, and suddenly I'm here on the couch and I can tear my eyes away from the photo at last.

"What?" I hear myself say.

"You looked like you got a chill," Nanaleen says.

"I'm okay," I say quickly. I say it again in my head, trying to convince myself: *I'm okay*. Without really meaning to, I look back at the photo.

There are only five kids in it. Just like there always were. There's no shadowy shape in the background.

I take a breath. It still feels like something inside me is rattling.

"Do you need another sweatshirt?" Nanaleen asks me.

I shake my head. "Is—?" I start to ask, without really knowing what I'm going to say.

But then Talia bursts into the room. She's waving her phone in one hand like she's the Statue of Liberty.

"I think your cell signal is broken," Talia says. "None of my texts are going through."

"Service is a little spotty out here," Nanaleen reminds her.

I'm okay, I tell myself one more time.

"Who're you even trying to text?" I ask.

Talia frowns at me like she's debating whether she has to answer that question. "My friend in town," she says.

"What friend?"

"You could call your friend on the landline," Nanaleen suggests. Talia makes a face like Nanaleen just suggested that she should spit in her own mug.

"No one *calls*," Talia says.

"Is it Inez?" Rose asks.

"Wait, your *nemesis* Inez?" I say.

"She's not my *nemesis*," Talia mutters, which means that yeah, it's her nemesis Inez. She's a girl around Talia's age whose family has started spending their summers in Misty Valley. The past two years, she's been here in July when we're visiting Nanaleen. The rest of the year, Inez goes to some STEM school an hour away from us and is captain of the robotics team that beat Talia's team at last year's state competition. Talia raged about it for a month.

"I thought she lived near Lexington," I say.

Talia's still fiddling with her phone. "She's here for fall break, too," she says.

I try not to be annoyed by that, but I am anyway. I'd figured that, for as many things as are wrong about this visit to Nanaleen's, at least Talia would be around for it. Just like she used to be. Talia, Rose, and I used to spend our visits to Misty Valley practically glued together. But two summers ago, when Inez came to town, Talia started ditching Rose and me to go hang out with Inez instead. They were always going swimming at the lake or spending whole afternoons nerding it up at the library. If Rose or I tried to tag along, Talia would frown at us and make up some reason to give us the boot.

Rose has never seemed as bothered by it as me, but Rose is just as happy sitting alone in a corner with a book as she is around other people. This past summer, Talia spent every single day glued to Inez instead of to either of us.

I'd always thought that me and my sisters had this unspoken agreement that we didn't really need other friends, especially not in Misty Valley. We had each other instead.

It turns out the agreement was unspoken because I'm the only one who agreed to it.

"I can call your friend's mom," Nanaleen tells

Talia now, trying again. "If you want to set up a playdate."

Talia groans. "Nobody has *playdates*, either."

"I have playdates," Rose says.

"Nobody over, like, age ten has playdates," Talia amends.

"We should finish the cinnamon rolls," I blurt out.

I guess I say it too loud, because they all stare at me for a second. I try to act like I don't notice. I want to be done with this conversation. The paused screen from Rose's show is still frozen on the TV: the group of deer, perked up and alerting each other about a threat. Getting ready to flee.

"Right?" I ask Nanaleen. "The dough's probably rested by now."

"I reckon so," Nanaleen says, and she finishes her tea in one big gulp before she pushes herself out of the recliner.

❋❋❋

In the kitchen, Nanaleen pulls out her two rolling pins: a boring metal one like the one Dad uses, and an antique one made of dark wood, with little ridges carved into its smooth, tapered handles. She waves the wooden one at me like a magic wand.

"This one was my mother's," she tells me.

"I know," I say, because she tells me that every time we bake. But I don't mind it. It feels like part of the baking process by now, and I'm especially glad for it in this moment, because it gives me something familiar to grab onto. Now that we're out of the living room, it's getting easier to convince myself I imagined that shadowy shape in the photo.

Nanaleen lets me use the rolling pin that was her mother's while she uses the boring metal one. We clean off the kitchen table again and then sprinkle flour all over it before we bring over the rested dough.

"You remember how to keep it from sticking?" Nanaleen asks me as we turn the dough out onto the tabletop.

"Lots of flour," I say, and I sprinkle around another handful of it.

"Exactly."

As we start rolling the dough out into a big rectangle, I try to imagine that we're in one of those old family photos—one of the black-and-white ones. I try to imagine that we're in a story like that, familiar and comfortable. One where you know the ending. I smooth out the dough with the same rolling pin Nanaleen's mom used back then, and I pretend our family now is as perfect as Nanaleen's was then. I try to imagine it so hard that it becomes true—the way I imagined myself into being Simon.

The imagining doesn't work as well on this, though. It still kind of feels like pretend.

Once Nanaleen decides that our rectangle of dough is wide enough, we spread the melted butter all over it and cover it with cinnamon sugar. Then we get to roll it up into a log. Nanaleen slices the log into individual rolls, all of them perfect spirals, and I line them up one by one in the baking pan.

"Make sure to leave space between them," Nanaleen reminds me. "They need room to rise."

I spread the rolls out a little more, giving them each a wide gap on all sides. Even after we've got them all in the baking pan, though, they look too small for the space. They look lonely. They're supposed to get bigger, I know—they'll rise if the yeast does its job right. But even though that part of the process always feels a little like magic, too, it's magic that hasn't happened yet.

We gather up all the dirty dishes we've used, and Nanaleen says we can just leave them beside the sink. She'll wash them later. As she picks up the rolling pins, she waves the old one at me again.

"You know, this one was my mother's," Nanaleen says.

I don't want to tell her that she already told me that today. I force a smile.

"I know," I say.

Dr. Skeffington and Company

SOMETIMES I WATCH THE OLD VIDEOS WE MADE A FEW SUMMERS ago—the year me, Talia, and Rose hunted ghosts here at Nanaleen's house. Talia had dug Nanaleen's ancient camcorder out of the basement, and we spent our whole month in Misty Valley pretending to be a research team that wanted to prove that the old O'Hagan house was haunted. The camcorder saved all the videos onto little tapes we could rewatch on Nanaleen's old VHS player, but after we went back home, Dad figured out how to turn all the tapes digital instead. He downloaded them all onto the computer, so now we can still watch everything we filmed that summer.

We all look so different in those videos. Younger. Talia's face was rounder back then, and it made all her expressions look more earnest and less prickly. Rose was only five or six, and her hair was wilder than ever. She's always running in and out of the frame on her little-kid legs, trying hard to be helpful.

"Look at this!" Rose yells on one of the videos. She's waving one hand out in front of her, but the camera's too shaky to see what she's holding. "The ESP is going wild!"

"You mean EMF," Talia says. "Electromagnetic frequency." I don't know where Talia had learned about EMF, but she pronounced the words like she'd been practicing saying them a lot. "It's supposed to spike when spirits are near," she adds.

"The EMF is going wild!" Rose tries again.

The camera finally steadies out, and it zooms in on her hand. She's not holding an EMF reader. She's holding Nanaleen's digital meat thermometer.

"Wow, you're right," Talia says solemnly. "Looks like the EMF is seventy-three degrees."

I don't show up on the screen very much, because I was usually holding the camera. Mostly you just hear my voice, too loud and too squeaky and sounding like it belongs to somebody else. I liked using the camcorder, though—even though Talia was always bossing me around about how to hold it better and where to point the lens.

In other home videos that we've made, sometimes my siblings call me by my old name and I have to fix it in my head. But on our ghost-hunting videos, it never comes up. During the game, they only ever called me by my character's name: Dr. Skeffington. Talia was Dr. Agatha Terror, the head of the research team and one of Dr. Skeffington's colleagues. Rose was their research assistant, Rose Raven. She was supposed to take notes about everything we found, but she couldn't really write yet, so most of her notes were scribbly doodles or words that Talia and I couldn't read.

The characters were my favorite part of the game. Talia liked having an excuse to scare Rose and me, and Rose just liked being included, I think.

But I liked pretending to be Dr. Skeffington. I never made up a first name for him that summer, but now, sometimes, I like to imagine that his first name was Simon.

Most of the videos from that summer are goofy and fun. They're just the three of us running around Nanaleen's house, pointing out a crooked picture frame or a line in the dust on one of Nanaleen's shelves. We claimed every single thing was evidence of ghosts. Nanaleen's house is really old, and it's easy to imagine ghosts haunting it. It's easy to pretend. We didn't plan on finding anything real.

At least I don't think we did.

But there's one video I always come back to when I'm clicking through them on the computer. We were filming in the second-floor hallway, which looks just the same now as it did in the old videos. Faded flowery wallpaper covers the walls. The wide trim along the baseboards is made of smooth wood—less shiny than it probably was when Nanaleen's grandfather first built the house, but still clean and nice. The hallway is always kind of dark, even during the day, because the light fixtures are high up and hard to reach. When the bulbs burn out, Nanaleen doesn't always replace them right away.

In the video, Talia is studying a little puddle on the floor in the middle of the hall. She's narrating in her Dr. Agatha Terror voice.

"It could be some kind of ectoplasm," she's saying, stroking her chin like she's deep in thought. "Sometimes ghosts leave that behind."

"Or it could be water somebody spilled from the bathroom," my too-loud voice says from behind the camera.

Rose peeks over Talia's shoulder to see. "Whoopsie," Rose says, wiping her hands on her overalls. "That was me."

Talia swats her away. "It's definitely ectoplasm. I'm sensing a lot of ghost activity around here. Dr. Skeffington, are you getting this?"

I'm pretty fidgety as a camera holder. In most of the videos, you only catch glimpses and flashes of the house in between blurry parts where I'm moving the camera. In this one, the camera swivels toward Talia and Rose, and then toward the puddle on the floor, and then down toward the end of the hallway, all in a row. Talia sighs.

"Skeffington," she says, annoyed. "Hold it still."

And then I do.

I'm not pointing it at Talia or Rose or the puddle, though. The camera's still pointing at the end of the hallway when it suddenly stops moving. I hold it there, frozen in place. If you turn up the volume, you can hear my breathing in the background.

"Skeffington," Talia says again. "What are you looking at?"

Afterward, whenever we've played the video back, Talia swears she doesn't see anything.

But sometimes, when I'm watching by myself, I pause the recording right at that moment. If I stare long enough at the end of the hall, where the overhead light is burned out, I start seeing a figure.

No, not a figure. An outline. An empty, person-shaped space.

Just like the thing that I maybe, possibly, probably saw in Nanaleen's black-and-white family photo.

Now, I can't remember why I pointed the camcorder at the end of the hallway when we were filming that day. I can't remember if I felt something there, or if I even noticed the figure while we were recording. Whenever we've rewatched the videos since then, whenever I've paused it at that moment and studied the frame, I've convinced myself afterward that I was probably imagining it.

I'm starting to think I wasn't imagining it.

What if our ghost-hunting game back then was like my secret name? Just because we thought it was imaginary when we started out, that doesn't mean it was.

What if it was more real than we knew?

HIDE-AND-SEEK

IT RAINS THIS AFTERNOON. FALL RAIN IS DIFFERENT THAN SUM-mer rain, I guess. When we usually visit Nanaleen, Misty Valley gets these big summer thunderstorms that drown the world for a couple of minutes at a time, and then they clear up, just like that. You wouldn't even know they'd happened afterward if it weren't for the puddles everywhere.

But this fall storm starts at lunchtime and keeps at it for the whole rest of the day. Sometimes it comes down in a drizzle, sometimes a downpour. Talia caved this morning and used Nanaleen's land-line to call Inez, but when the rain starts, she has to stay home instead of walking into town to meet her.

I know it's just weather, but secretly I wonder if I somehow willed the storm to happen to make Talia stay home and hang out with us instead of Inez.

If I did, I don't feel bad about it.

Nanaleen tells us she needs to rest her eyes for a little while, which really means she's going to take a nap in her room while she listens to one of her murder mystery audiobooks. Talia looks like she might go back to texting and being boring, and Rose starts to sneak off with one of her books, but I pester both of them until they agree to play hide-and-seek instead.

We've played hide-and-seek at Nanaleen's house so many times that it's nearly impossible to find a new hiding spot. We've used all the good ones already. At least one of us has hidden under every bed, behind every curtain, inside every closet and cubby. Talia figured out a while back how to hide herself under the dining room table by lying down on the pushed-in chairs so you can't see her under the tablecloth. Rose once managed to climb inside

Nanaleen's linen closet and wedge herself all the way up on the top shelf. When I'd tried to climb up to tag her, we'd both gone tumbling down in a pile of clean bedsheets and towels.

Nanaleen wasn't thrilled about that one.

This round, I decide to hide in the closet in the history room. The history room has a bed in it, technically, but no one ever sleeps here, because the bed is covered in old photos waiting to be sorted and put into their albums. The albums are one of Nanaleen's projects. I guess she has to do something besides bake and clean and listen to murder mysteries when she doesn't have us here visiting. She spends hours in here sometimes, lining photos up on the old bedspread and writing Post-it notes with information to help her find the right year for them.

I spy a couple of the Post-its as I sneak through the history room to get to the closet. The notes are written in the same cramped, slanting cursive from her recipe card.

Mother with her choir group—1954 or '55?

What year was Denny baptized?

Holy Cross Church renovation—when did it finish?

The family has been in one place for enough generations that parts of Nanaleen's family history can double up as a local history. In the backgrounds of all the albums, you can see Misty Valley changing over the last century. Sometimes, Nanaleen will have one of us kids pick a year, and then she'll pull that year's album off the shelf and sit us all down and flip through the pages with us, telling us about each photo.

Now, I tug open the door to the history room's closet and wedge myself inside.

The history room's closet is stuffed with even more family history. But it's a different kind. Nanaleen uses this closet for storage, which means it's full of plastic dry cleaning bags holding Mom's and her sisters' old prom dresses and clothes they outgrew but never got rid of. Some of the clothes are even older. To get inside, I have to push past a heavy wool coat that smells like dust and a brown leather jacket that's worn so soft, the leather feels like velvet. The floor of the closet is lined with boxes of toys Mom and my aunts played with when they were little. Talia, Rose, and I used to play with them, too, when we visited, but most of them are little-kid stuff.

Talia's *it* for this round, and she's sure to come looking inside the closet. I squeeze myself into the back corner where I hope she won't be able to see me when she opens the doors, and then I bury myself in a pile of old stuffed animals. There have to be at least thirty of them. Some are leaking cotton or missing their little plastic eyeballs. When we were younger, Nanaleen would have each of us kids pick out one of the stuffies to sleep with while we were visiting. But only Rose still does that now.

By the time I hear Talia finish counting, I've hidden myself in a mountain of stuffies with only my face uncovered. I grab a floppy dog that Rose used to love and prop it over my face. Or maybe it's a bear. I can't really tell. Rose always called it Fuzzle Mouth. I can still see a sliver of dark closet from under Fuzzle Mouth's armpit, but otherwise I'm buried.

And then I wait.

The waiting is the worst part of hide-and-seek. As soon as I have to stay still, it's like my whole body remembers that it wants to move. My hands want to fidget and my legs want to twitch. The longer I don't move, the worse it gets, and soon my legs start feeling weird and heavy, like if I don't let them do something, they're going to fall off.

That's when I hear the landline phone ring.

There's a shuffling sound from downstairs, and a door opening; Nanaleen must've gotten up from her nap to answer the phone. There's a click from the kitchen. The ringing stops.

Nanaleen's voice answers, and then there's a pause. Then she says, "Of course! Just a minute, let me get the kids on."

And I know right then that it's Mom or Dad calling.

✳✳✳

My parents met each other on their first day of college. Dad was an English major; Mom was studying art history, which she teaches now. The University of Louisville is big enough that they might not have ever met, except that they got put on the same campus orientation tour on that first day and got to talking. They became friends, and then they became boyfriend and girlfriend, and then after they graduated, they got married. Easy as that.

Nanaleen said once that their romance was so perfect, it was like something out of a movie. I've always thought she's got it wrong, though. Movies have to have conflict: lots of ups and downs, problems to sort out, stuff getting in the way. A romance can't be both perfect *and* like something out of a movie. A perfect romance would be pretty boring to watch.

I wish Mom and Dad would've stayed boring.

Nanaleen hollers up the stairs for us kids to come to the phone, but I don't move. Is it Mom or Dad? Maybe Mom is calling on her lunch break in between her Monday classes. Maybe Dad got lonely in the house by himself and is giving up on job-searching for the day.

It could be both of them together, I guess. But probably not.

Nanaleen is chatting with whichever of them

it is while she waits for me and Talia and Rose. I can't hear every word through the floorboards, but I can catch pieces. Based on how normal Nanaleen sounds, you wouldn't know about her smile slipping this morning. You wouldn't guess that anything's wrong—not with her, and not with whichever of our parents she's talking to.

"Simon and I did a little baking this morning," Nanaleen is telling them. "He's turning into a pretty good chef."

Except she doesn't say "Simon," and she doesn't say "he"—of course she doesn't. I fix the name and pronoun in my head, just like always, and I feel the quickest spark of annoyance, just like always, even though it's not Nanaleen's fault because she doesn't know. Because I haven't told her.

But this time, it's like the spark catches. It flares up all at once, like when you light a stove, and suddenly the anger is spreading all the way through me. Burning me up. It's the fast, overwhelming kind of angry that feels like you need to hit a pillow, or hit the wall, or break something. Or scream.

It's not her fault, I say in my head, over and over. *She doesn't know any better. You haven't* told *her. There's no reason to be mad.*

Knowing that doesn't make it stop, but I clench my hands into fists and then clench them again and then breathe in and out, slow. And I push it down. I push the mad back where it belongs.

I don't climb out of the closet to go talk to Mom or Dad.

I stay put.

Here's what I can tell Nanaleen later on, so she won't wonder about what's wrong: *Oh, sorry, I didn't hear you calling for us. No, that's okay. I'll talk to them next time.*

If it's Dad on the phone, he can just blame it on my selective hearing again.

Or maybe I'll say that I didn't want to stop in the middle of a round of hide-and-seek. I can say that I didn't know we were pausing our game, even though I can hear Rose down in the kitchen now, out from her hiding spot. I can hear snippets of her half of the conversation on the landline. She's talking about the deer from her show again.

I huddle down deeper under my pile of stuffed animals instead, and I try my best not to think.

The problem with *not* thinking is that the harder you try, the more you think. As soon as I tell myself not to think, my brain starts darting around like a dog out for a walk, trying to get off its leash. It starts racing toward thinking about Mom and Dad, and about their reset, and I grip the leash as tight as I can. It works for a second. It starts slowing down. But then it starts jumping around toward Nanaleen using my old name, and I try to tug it back again, and then as soon as I start getting it back under control it takes off toward Nanaleen's slipping smiles. And I have to wrangle it all over again.

It's like I'm in a fight with my own mind. It's exhausting.

My head feels too full, and I wiggle my toes inside my socks just to be doing something else, feeling something else. The closet is totally dark. Totally cold. I've got a blanket of stuffed animals stacked over me, but for some reason goose bumps are still rising up my arms under my hoodie. That's easier to focus on than any of the things inside my brain. I shudder, just like I did earlier when I saw the shadowy shape in the photo. I can't see a thing in here. It's so dark that the figure I've imagined on our old ghost-hunting videos—the figure I saw—could be right in front of me and I wouldn't know it. It could be hovering right over my shoulder, just like the shadowy outline that hovered behind Nanaleen's shoulder in her old family photo.

The shadowy figure could be right outside the closet door.

Slowly, slowly, all the hairs up the back of my neck stand on end.

There's a sound somewhere nearby—nearer than the voices downstairs. So near that it's like it's inside the wall right beside me. It's soft. Almost imaginary, but not quite.

Scritch-scritch-scritch.

I stop wiggling my toes in case I'm the one making the sound. For a second, everything is quiet. I try to breathe. My heart is thudding in my chest.

Then it happens again. *Scritch-scritch-scritch.*

Just like that, I know it's the shadowy figure.

Run, my brain says. But I'm stuck. Frozen.

The sour smell of the house, the smell I noticed yesterday when we first got here, hasn't faded yet. It's stronger than ever. Once, Talia left a pair of wet, muddy socks in Dad's car for a week in the middle of August, and it smelled almost exactly like this. The stink of it seeped into everything for months.

Run, my brain tries again.

I think about the deer on Rose's show, standing at alertness, poised to flee from the danger but not fleeing yet. Paused on the screen in that moment. My body's frozen, put on pause, but I know somehow that the empty shape isn't. It's closing in.

Open the closet door, my brain says. *It'll be less scary in the light. Open the door and run downstairs to where everybody else is.*

But the smell just gets stronger, and the scratching just gets louder, and I can *feel* the figure right outside the door now. Waiting for me.

A click. The closet door flies open.

It's a miracle I don't scream. I clamp my jaw shut

and squint my eyes in the sudden light streaming inside and keep Fuzzle Mouth up over my face, like somehow he might save me from the shadowy, terrifying thing that's coming for me.

But it isn't the shadowy figure. It's Talia.

Relief hits me in a wave. Talia is shuffling the dry cleaning bags and old jackets back and forth on the rail above me, easy as anything. If that thing—whatever it is—really was outside the closet a second ago, she's totally unaware of it. She moves a box and peeks behind it, and then she turns toward my stuffie pile.

I sense the exact moment when she spots me buried there.

"*There* you are," she says. "Come on, Mom's on the phone."

My brain starts running in different directions again, trying to get off its leash. I try wiggling my toes again. I want to *move*.

But my heart's still pounding from sensing that thing outside the door, and I can't. I stay put.

"Simon, I can see you," Talia says again, annoyed. "Come on."

Any second now, she's going to ask *why* I'm not coming downstairs—she's going to want to know what's wrong. *Everything's fine*, I tell myself. *Everything's totally fine.*

I wiggle Fuzzle Mouth's paws a little bit, trying to make it look like he's waving up at Talia from in front of my face.

"I don't know who you're talking about," I say in a squeaky voice. "I'm not Simon. I'm Fuzzle Mouth."

Talia snorts. "Right. I should've known."

"The round's not over," I make Fuzzle Mouth say.

"Okay, well, it's over now, 'cause I found you. Come on."

She reaches a hand into the closet to help me up, or maybe just to tag me. It happens in slow motion. I *need* to move. I picture my route in my mind, clear enough to make it real: out into the hallway, down the stairs, across the living room to the built-in bench by the window. It's what we always use as home base when we play hide-and-seek. Talia's got me trapped, blocking the closet door, but I've gotten out of trickier spots than this.

Even with the closet door open, even in the

light, I can feel the shadowy shape still somewhere nearby. Closing in.

"It's not over till you tag me!" I yell all in a rush, and then I throw Fuzzle Mouth straight at Talia's face.

Talia yelps like a startled pterodactyl and jumps backward. Just far enough for me to get past her. I dive out of my stuffie pile and scramble under her arms. Talia tries to throw Fuzzle Mouth back at me, but she misses, and he hits the doorframe beside my head right as I run through it. Talia's spitting behind me like she might've gotten some fuzzle in *her* mouth, but she's also laughing.

"You won't get away with this!" she yells, like I'm some cartoon villain she's trying to capture, and that gets me laughing, too. I imagine her shaking her fists at me. But I'm already in the hallway. I sprint toward the stairs, slipping in my socks on the hardwood floor.

Running feels good. It feels right. My brain isn't thinking about anything at all now. I'm breathing hard, and my pumping heart clears that angry feeling from earlier right back out of me. Talia's hot on my heels, but not close enough to grab me. At the top of the staircase, I grab onto the banister and swing myself onto the stairs.

The staircase down to the main floor curves around and then points straight into the living room. The bench that's our home base is right across from it, right in sight at the bottom. I can see Nanaleen there in the living room doorway, and Rose right behind her. Rose has the landline phone clutched in her hand.

Three things happen all in a row, so fast they're almost simultaneous:

One: I hurl myself down the staircase. I'm moving too fast to stop, and even if I *could* slow myself down, I probably wouldn't.

Two: Something presses into the middle of my back. A cold pressure right between my shoulder blades. Like a hand. For a second I think Talia must have caught me, but she's not even on the stairs yet—I'm way out of her reach.

Three: The hand gives me a shove, and that push is all it takes for me to tip forward. I overbalance. My foot slips off the stair I was aiming for and lands in empty air.

And then I'm falling.

Guardian Angels

WHEN I WAS LITTLE, MOM TAUGHT US ALL HOW TO PRAY TO OUR guardian angels. She printed a prayer out on a page from the computer and put it in a frame in the bedroom we all share at home. It's still there, hanging on the wall. Sometimes, when she and Dad would come tuck us all in for the night, Mom would read it out for us.

Oh Angel of God, my guardian dear,
To whom God's love commits me here:
Ever this day, be at my side
To light, to guard, to rule, to guide. Amen.

After she'd read it, she'd kiss me on the forehead, and then Talia, and then Rose, and then Dad would do the same. And then they'd turn out the light—and I would lie in the dark for hours imagining a guardian angel hiding somewhere in our bedroom. Guardian angels are supposed to be good, protective. They're supposed to watch over you to keep you safe. I knew Mom's prayer was supposed to be comforting.

But it's always kind of freaked me out.

I don't know whether I believe that guardian angels are real. I don't know if Mom does, either. I don't really like the idea of some angel following me around all the time, watching everything I do.

Nanaleen has statues of angels all around her house: pink-cheeked and golden-haired, with harps and fluffy wings that could have come out of a cartoon. All the statues' faces are so serene, so calm.

Even if guardian angels *are* real, I'm pretty sure they don't look like Nanaleen's statues. If there's an angel whose job it is to try to keep me out of trouble at every turn, they'd probably look a lot more frazzled than that.

✳✳✳

I don't remember the actual moment of falling down the stairs. Just one second I realize I'm going to, and the next I'm sprawled on the living room floor.

All the air inside me has been pushed to the outside. My feet are splayed out over the bottom step. My forehead's burning, and my brain manages to pull back a split-second memory from the lost moment: my head smacking against the floor as I landed.

Maybe it's not a memory, not really. Maybe I'm just putting together what must've happened and convincing myself that I remember it.

"Lord Almighty!" Nanaleen is saying from somewhere.

"Oh my gosh," Talia's voice says, and I can tell that she almost said "God" and then changed it at the last second for Nanaleen's sake, even though Nanaleen already said "Lord."

"We're gonna have to call you back," Rose says into the phone in a flat voice. And then she hangs up on Mom.

86

I try not to breathe out in relief at that, but I do a little. I still feel like I've missed a second. It's like the mornings when Talia turns on the lights in our bedroom before I'm really awake, and for that first moment everything is too bright and not real and I don't know where I am. I try to sit up. Talia's made it down the stairs behind me, and she crouches on the bottom step now, peering down at me.

"Are you okay?" she asks.

"Yeah." My voice sounds like I'm trying to inhale a frog, so I take a couple deep breaths. Remind my lungs how to work. Slowly prop myself up on my elbows. "Yeah, I'm good."

"Lord Almighty," Nanaleen says again, shaking her head. "Anything broken? Anything hurt?" She takes my arms one at a time and examines them, then tips my chin up to check my face. "You've got a goose egg up here already." She nods at my forehead. I rub it.

"I'm fine, really." The shock of it is wearing off now, and I sit up all the way. Nanaleen tries to check my arms again and I brush her off.

"You landed, like, two inches from the fire-place," Talia says, and that's when I realize her voice is a little bit shaky. "Two more inches and..."

We all look at the living room fireplace right beside me. Just beyond the foot of the stairs. The hearth is made of rusty brown bricks that are original to the house, and they stretch almost to the spot I landed in. The spot where my head hit the floor. I can't stop looking at the corner of the brick there, jagged and solid and very, very sharp.

Two more inches and...

My insides are jumping all around now. In my mind, I keep seeing what could have happened: me landing two inches farther away, hitting my forehead on that jagged fireplace edge, busting my head open. I try to reach the spot in the middle of my back where I felt something push me. The cold hand.

The spot feels normal now.

I take a deep breath, and then I make myself look up the staircase to the place where it happened.

There's nothing there.

Nanaleen has puffed out her cheeks, and now she lets out a long, rattling breath. I don't like the way she's looking at me, and I don't like the way Talia's voice shook. I can tell I worried both of them. Badly.

I'm not supposed to worry anyone.

"I'm okay, Nanaleen," I say again, and I make myself smile big and wave my hands a little like that helps prove it. I'm trying to convince her, and I guess I'm also trying to convince myself, even though everything inside me feels just as rattled as Nanaleen looks. "Seriously."

Nanaleen nods a little, and she pats my cheek, and she looks up at the heavy wood mantel that hangs over the fireplace. Two of her angel statues are perched on it. She's been collecting the statues for longer than I've been alive, and the two on the mantel are probably older than me. They're painted ceramic, both of them in billowing blue robes. They smile down at us.

"All right, then," Nanaleen says. "All right. I'll thank your guardian angel for keeping you safe."

Goose Egg

NANALEEN BUNDLES ME UP ON THE COUCH WITH A GLASS OF water and an ice pack pressed to my forehead. She gets the TV set up on a cartoon I haven't watched since I was little, and she keeps patting my cheek, like she's still making sure I'm not going to die. Talia's hovering around just like her. She keeps asking if I'm sure I'm okay, again and again. It makes me think of one time a couple years back, when I scraped up my knee on the sidewalk outside our house and Talia sat with me while I cried and then helped me clean it up and cover it with a Spider-Man Band-Aid, and the whole time, she didn't even complain or call me a baby.

I let them get me settled in. I let them take care of me, just like I know I'm supposed to, and I keep smiling and reassuring them that I'm all right. My heart's still beating pretty fast, though, and my brain's running all over the place. I keep touching the spot on my back where I felt the hand push me. Even when I move my hand away from it, the skin under my sweatshirt there feels tingly and alert, like it's remembering the touch. The ghost of a touch.

A ghost.

"Y'all are going to have to find something else to do this week besides running around the house like hooligans," Nanaleen is saying. "I promised your parents I'd return you in one piece, and I intend to do that."

"Wouldn't we be in three pieces?" Rose asks. "Since there are three of us?" Nanaleen frowns at her, but Rose really isn't trying to mouth off, I don't think. I think she's genuinely asking. Nanaleen sighs.

"Yes, all right. As many pieces as you came here in."

"Sorry, Nanaleen," I say. "We'll be more careful."

"*I* was being careful," Talia says.

"I'm always careful," Rose says.

"No more hide-and-seek," Nanaleen tells us. "Not in the house, at least. No more running around."

"What?" I blurt out louder than I mean to. Outside the front window, the rain's still coming down, pattering against the glass in a little tap-dancing rhythm. It doesn't show any signs of stopping. "No *running*?"

"You heard me," Nanaleen says. "Somebody's going to lose a limb."

It seems like an overreaction considering I didn't even break anything—no bones, no furniture, nothing. I didn't even break any of Nanaleen's angel figurines. I open my mouth to argue with her.

But Talia shoots me a frown, and I hear Mom's voice in my head: *Don't make trouble, okay?*

I clamp my mouth shut again.

"We should call your mom back," Nanaleen says. "Let her know what happened. She's probably worried."

My arms and legs have started getting heavy again, like they did while I was hiding upstairs and trying to stay still. Every part of me wants to move. *Needs* to move. It's not enough to nod my head and agree to talk to Mom; my whole self wants to jump off the couch now and take off running and not stop.

There's a tickling feeling against my back, right in that same spot. Fingers running up my spine. I jerk away from it and try to snap my head around, try to check behind me.

There's no one there.

Of course there isn't. Nanaleen and Talia and Rose are all still standing in front of me, all in plain sight. None of them could have reached me. No one is behind me.

So why do I still feel like I'm being watched?

Ghost.

"Simon?" Nanaleen says. "Do you feel up to talking with your mom?"

Something about her voice tells me it's not the first time she asked. I don't know how long I've been sitting here without answering. My mind's still jumping in so many directions: the ghostly hand, and my throbbing forehead, and the scratching sound I heard in the closet upstairs, and the musty smell that's still all around us, and the shadowy figure. And then Mom on the other end of the phone line when Nanaleen calls her back. Mom wanting to hear all about how our vacation has been going so far, which means more smiling and more reassuring people that I'm fine.

"Simon?" Talia says, and she doesn't sound at all annoyed with me now. I still wish I wasn't worrying anyone—but I have to admit that I'd rather have Talia worrying about me instead of rolling her eyes or ignoring me to text with Inez.

"I'm kind of worn out," I say finally. "Can I just talk to her tomorrow?"

Nanaleen tells me yes, of course, Mom will understand, and she makes me peel back the ice pack so she can check the goose egg on my forehead again. She has a deep line between her eyebrows like the one Rose gets, except that Nanaleen's line makes her look concerned instead of crabby.

"You're going to have quite a lump up there," Nanaleen tells me. She only lets me poke at the spot for a couple of seconds before she swats my hand away and tells me to leave it be. Then she checks the ice pack, which is starting to get warm. "I'll go swap this out. Stay put, you hear?"

She ruffles my hair on the way out of the room. I like how it feels now that my hair is short—straight brown strands that tickle my head and stick however Nanaleen tousles them. I wait till she's in the kitchen before I feel my forehead again. I've had goose eggs before, but I've never really thought about why Nanaleen calls them that until now. The one I got today is big enough that it really does feel like an egg swelling up under my skin.

"I think the swelling is supposed to be a good thing, though," Talia says. She's leaning on the arm of the couch beside me, and she's still watching me closely. "It means the blood has someplace to go, right?"

Rose nods, perking up in that way she does when she's talking about a book she's read. "You'd rather have a lump on the outside than swelling on the inside," she agrees.

I only spend a second picturing the goose

egg on the inside of my head, squeezing against my brain, before I get a squeamish feeling in my gut. Better to put that on the always-growing list of things not to think too hard about. I can hear Nanaleen digging through the freezer, and I know she'll be back any second. I grab Rose's and Talia's hands and pull them in close to me.

"Sibling Conference," I say in a low voice. "Upstairs. Five minutes."

Talia blinks down at me, and for a second I think she's going to refuse. We haven't done a Sibling Conference in a long time—probably not since Talia started middle school. Sibling Conference might be the kind of thing that makes Talia sigh and roll her eyes now.

But finally she nods, and Rose nods, and they both say they'll meet me up in the Dormitory.

I don't know what it was that pushed me down the stairs. But I know that something did.

And I know it wasn't my guardian angel.

Sibling Conference

WE'VE BEEN PLAYING SIBLING CONFERENCE FOR AGES, PROBABLY for as long as Rose has been able to talk in full sentences. It's a pretty basic game. One of us just announces that we're having a Sibling Conference, and then me and Talia and Rose all have to sit cross-legged on the floor and hold each other's hands in a circle while whoever called the conference goes over the day's business. It's a very formal process, even though we usually use it for goofy, informal things, like picking what movie we want to watch on our Friday movie nights, or planning out Mom's birthday gift.

At Nanaleen's house, we always do Sibling

Conference up in the Dormitory. Usually it's because the Dormitory is one of the few places in the house where the grown-ups won't hear us. Without Mom and Dad here, there are plenty of other places we could meet while avoiding Nanaleen. But we stick with the Dormitory out of tradition.

It takes me a while to convince Nanaleen to let me off the couch, and then she's still watching me, so I have to walk instead of running up the stairs two at a time like I usually do. By the time I make it to the attic, Talia and Rose are already assembled, sitting in the middle of the floor. Rose is cross-legged. Talia's tipped back with her head on the floorboards, typing on her phone again. I guess her worrying over me has worn off.

"That was more than five minutes," Rose tells me as I plop down in my spot beside her.

"Well, I'm here now," I say. "Talia?"

"Just a sec," Talia says without looking away from the screen. She's holding her phone straight above her head. If she dropped it for some reason, it would land smack on her nose, or maybe her forehead. I wonder if she's texting with Inez again. Maybe she's telling Inez about Sibling Conference—but as soon as I think it, I know she's not. Talia never used to be embarrassed by our games, but she is now. Or maybe she's just embarrassed by Rose and me.

Talia finally finishes texting. She sits up and then tosses her phone across the room and onto her mattress. It almost bounces off and smashes on the floor, but her pillow catches it instead.

"Okay," Talia says, finally looking at me. "What's up?"

"Wait," Rose says. "Not yet."

"Why?" Talia says.

"We haven't called the meeting to order."

Rose takes the rules of Sibling Conference very seriously. Talia used to—she was the one who made up most of the rules in the first place. Once, she even wrote an oath for us all to recite at the beginning of each meeting. (Rose was too little to remember it all, though, and she cried whenever she forgot the words, so we stopped doing that part.)

"Fine, you do it," Talia tells her, and Rose takes a deep breath.

Rose holds out her hands on either side of her, palms up, wrists resting on her knees. I grab one of her hands and reach out to Talia the same way. Talia sighs, like she wasn't the one who invented this part of Sibling Conference. Like just a couple of years ago she wasn't the one squealing at us that we had to hold hands during it. But finally she takes Rose's hand and mine. She finishes out the circle.

"I hereby call this meeting to order," Rose says. Then she nods at me. "Okay. You can go."

I take a deep breath and say, "I think a ghost pushed me down the stairs."

Talia laughs.

Rose and I don't. Talia stops laughing when she realizes we haven't joined her. The laugh flickers and dims like the overhead lights do whenever Nanaleen's furnace kicks on. Then it burns out.

"What?" Talia says.

"You heard me. I think a ghost pushed me down the stairs and Nanaleen's house is haunted."

"*What?*" Talia says again.

"Wait," Rose says, "wait. Go back. Why do you think a ghost pushed you down the stairs?"

I tell them about the hand that shoved me in the back when I was running away from Talia. Talia frowns.

"I didn't push you, I swear," she says, totally missing the point.

"Exactly," I say. "But something did."

"Or maybe you just tripped because you were running too fast."

Frustration snakes through me, just a little bit. I try to push it back. "I didn't *trip*."

"Okay, but I was right behind you," Talia says. "There was nothing there."

"Nothing you could *see*," I say.

"And that's why you think it was a ghost?" Rose asks. She doesn't say it doubtfully, though—I think she's just clarifying.

"That's part of it, yeah," I say, and then, before I can lose my nerve, I add, "I've been sensing this . . . presence."

Slowly, I try to explain to them about the thing I thought I felt lurking outside the closet door when we were playing hide-and-seek. And about the shadowy outline I saw in Nanaleen's old photo. And about the shape I think we caught on camera back during our ghost-hunting game years ago. Even before I start telling them the details, Talia's eyebrows are pulled low and skeptical, and the more I talk, the lower they keep inching. She doesn't believe me. I already can tell. Rose is nodding slowly, keeping an open mind, at least, but Talia doesn't believe any of this.

I wish I could have Talia on my side instead of Rose. Right away I feel bad for thinking it. But that doesn't change the truth.

When I'm finished talking, they both just sit there for a long moment. The quiet bites at me.

"Look, Simon...," Talia starts to say. But my old name combined with the bored, *haven't we done this before?* voice she's using makes that little frustrated piece inside me grow into a *big* frustrated piece all at once.

"No, *you* look," I cut in. "Haven't you felt it? Haven't you felt how there's something different here this trip? Everything feels different."

Talia shakes her head. "That's just because Mom and Dad aren't here."

"It's been colder than usual," I say Temperature changes can be a sign of hauntings sometimes; I remember that from when we played as Dr. Skeffington and his team.

"Because it's fall instead of summer," Talia points out.

"And the house *smells* different. Haven't you noticed the smell?"

"I did think it smelled kind of funny yesterday," Rose says.

"Don't tell me you're believing this, Miss Science," Talia snaps at her. If Talia were glaring at me like that, I'd probably back down immediately and apologize a dozen times, even if I wasn't really sorry, just to get her to stop. But Rose barely even seems to notice the glare.

"Science just means you make a hypothesis

103

and then test it," Rose says evenly, like she's reciting back something she read in one of her books. "That's how you figure out what's true and what isn't. Simon has a hypothesis, so..."

"Exactly," I say, nodding. "So we test it. We can gather evidence, or whatever."

I don't realize how tightly I've been clenching both of their hands till Talia pulls hers out of my grip. She shakes her fingers loose and massages her palm a little.

"You're not going to find *evidence* that Nanaleen's house is haunted," Talia says.

"I've already got some stuff that *might* be evidence, though, right?" I say. "We should make a list."

"You're not going to find evidence because *ghosts aren't real.*"

But Rose has already broken our hand circle even more and is crawling over to her bed to dig through the pile of books beside it. She comes back a few seconds later carrying a pencil and one of her notebooks—a sparkly purple one with a unicorn on the front that Mom got her for the new school year. She pushes them both at Talia.

"You write it," Rose says.

Talia wrinkles her nose. "Why me?"

"Because I write too slow and Simon writes too messy. Please?"

Rose screws up her face into this pitiful, puppy-dog-eyed look that she knows Talia can't say no to. I've tried to use that face on Talia sometimes, but mine's not as good as Rose's. Talia says when I do it, I just look like I have gas.

Talia tips her head back and groans at the ceiling, and then she tips her head forward again and sighs at the floor. And then she accepts the pencil and notebook from Rose and smooths it open on the floor on a blank page.

She writes at the top of the page: *Signs That Nanaleen's House Is Haunted.*

"I just want it on the record that I don't believe in this stuff," Talia says as she draws a line underneath the title.

"Fine," I say. "Let the record show that Talia's

a nonbeliever. And also let the record show that Talia is wrong."

Talia snorts a laugh and then cuts it off like she didn't mean for it to come out. She writes: *Shadowy creepy figure (alleged).*

"What's al...leg...ed?" Rose asks, sounding out the word even though she's reading it upside-down.

"It's when someone *claims* something happened," Talia says. "But you don't know if it really did yet."

She gives me a pointed look, because it's clear I'm the *someone* here. I squinch up my nose at her. She keeps writing:

Invisible something that pushed Simon down the stairs (alleged)

Scratching sound inside the wall (alleged)

Changes in temperature (alleged)

"Put the bad smell down," I say.

"That one's not alleg-ed," Rose says, even though I think she's still saying the word wrong. "I smelled it, too."

"Just because it's there doesn't mean it's because of ghosts," Talia says. But she writes *Bad smell*, and she doesn't put any parentheses after it.

It's not a very long list, but seeing it all written out makes my insides settle down a little at last. It makes everything on the list feel more real, even if Talia doesn't think so. Talia slams the pencil down and shoves the notebook back across the floor to Rose.

"There," Talia says. "Are we done now?"

Already she's glancing back at her phone lying faceup on her bed—the screen's lit up with another text. Probably from Inez. I wish we hadn't let go of each other's hands. I want to grab Talia's hand and hold her in place. Even when we're doing Sibling Conference just like we always have, Talia's only halfway here.

"What's our action item?" Rose asks. That's another of the rules of Sibling Conference: We always have to end by picking an action item, something specific we're going to do about it after the meeting's over. Whenever Mom does work calls from home, that's how her boss always ends meetings.

"I think we should restart our ghost-hunting game," I say.

Talia and Rose both just stare at me. I stare right back, squaring my shoulders, trying to stand my ground even though we're sitting. I keep thinking about the old videos, about the three of us kids wandering all around Nanaleen's house, pointing at things and goofing off together and talking about ghosts. I think I've known what I wanted to be today's action item from the very beginning, from when I first told them to meet me up here.

"We don't have to use our pretend names or anything," I add, because I get this needling feeling that Talia's about to complain about that. "We don't have to *pretend* at all. But we can borrow the camcorder again, and we can go room to room, and we can look for evidence. *Real* evidence this time."

Talia sighs again. It's a long, drawn-out sigh, and it sounds older than hers usually do, like she wants to roll her eyes at me but is holding it in.

She's trying to show she's above all this, I realize. Trying to be the grown-up, even though she's only two years older than me.

"Look," she says. "I get that you're shaken up from..." She nods at the goose egg on my forehead, and I rub it, like maybe I can hide the bruising underneath.

"This isn't just because I'm shaken up," I say.

"And I know things are...weird right now. Mom and Dad—"

"Things are *weird*," I cut in before she can finish that sentence, "because we're staying in a haunted house."

My leg is jiggling, bouncing up and down, just like it nearly always does if I'm not actively telling it not to. Talia's eyes dart down at it and then back at my face, and I think she's going to tell me to stop, but she doesn't. So I just look her in the eyes and let it keep bouncing.

"We have to vote," Rose says, carefully, like she thinks either one of us might explode at any moment. "On the action item."

Talia's mouth pinches down, but finally, she looks away. "Fine," she says at last. "All in favor of restarting the ghost-hunting game?"

I shoot my hand up, even faster than I do when my teacher Mrs. Ikeda asks for volunteers to carry the school equipment bag outside for PE. Rose hesitates for just a second, and then she raises her hand, too. She gives me a little smile like she's excited to be on my team.

I make myself smile back, and I try not to wish I had my other sister on my team instead.

The Feeling in the Dark

IT RAINS FOR THE WHOLE REST OF THE DAY—ALL THROUGH suppertime, and all evening while we play checkers and Connect Four around Nanaleen's coffee table. I only play one round, and then, when Talia decides we should set up a tournament, I tell everybody I just want to watch instead. Nanaleen and Talia give me those soft, worried looks again, and I know they're both figuring I'm sitting out because my head still hurts. Which it does.

But really, I'm sitting out so I don't have to play against Rose, because Rose can usually beat me in both checkers *and* Connect Four. And it's really embarrassing to lose over and over again to your baby sister.

Dad calls right before bed. I don't really want to talk to him, but I already skipped talking with Mom today. If I say I'm not up for a phone call now, either...I guess I'd rather put on my *everything's great* voice and talk to Dad for five minutes than have Nanaleen and both my parents fussing at me.

"Hey, kiddo," Dad says after Nanaleen gives me the phone. "I hear you had quite the afternoon." I guess Mom told him about my fall down the stairs. Maybe they really are getting more time to talk this week without us kids around.

"It was all good," I tell him.

"Sounds like you had a close call," he says.

"Nah," I say like it's no big deal. "Nanaleen just worries."

"Well, I'm glad you're okay. We've got enough going on without..." He laughs, but it's in that short, tense way he does when he's trying too hard to keep everything light and breezy. He's been doing that laugh a lot lately. "How's your head feeling?"

My forehead throbs like the goose egg just got woken up, but I say, "Totally fine. All better."

And then we talk about nothing for a few minutes.

I mean, we talk about *things*—I tell him about the cinnamon rolls we made, and Dad tells me about this funny sign he saw outside the grocery store this morning, and we talk about the weather. Louisville is getting the same rain we are, I guess.

But we don't talk about anything important. I don't tell him about our Sibling Conference or that Rose and I are going to restart our ghost-hunting game. He doesn't tell me whether he and Mom have had enough time to talk yet or how their "reset" is going.

So those are the things I'm trying not to think about when we all go to bed. For hours I lie there in the dark, listening to the rain, staring up at the slanting Dormitory ceiling.

There's a brownish stain on the ceiling right above my bed. It's been there for years, for as long as I can remember. Probably forever. Once upon a time, the roof of the old O'Hagan house sprung a leak, I guess, and the rainwater that seeped through left a sprawling, rusty stain on the drywall ceiling. The roof's been fixed for a long time now. It doesn't leak anymore, even when the rain pounds down on it the way it has been today.

The stain is still there, though. Tonight, I stare up at that brownish spot and try to find different shapes in its outline. This is the game I play whenever I can't fall asleep at Nanaleen's house—which is usually, but to be fair, I usually can't fall asleep at home, either. Finding shapes in the water stain helps for the same reason people count sheep, I think. It helps to have just one thing to try to focus on.

But when I try to concentrate on the water stain, I'm fighting against my own brain again. Part of the brown spot stretches out into a kind of crescent, almost like a smile, and just like that, I'm thinking about Dad's trying-too-hard laugh on the phone. About how he was working so hard to keep things light, which means things aren't light. There's an anxious knot forming in my chest, but I push it down and try to find a different shape on the ceiling.

If I look close enough in the middle of the water stain, I can find a kind of rectangle, and then I'm thinking about the sharp corner of the fireplace earlier, and how close my head came to hitting it. I'm remembering Dad's comment that he has enough going on already, and the looks Talia and Nanaleen have been giving me.

Tomorrow, I decide, I'll be extra friendly and cheerful and happy. Tomorrow I'll show them that I'm totally fine, and that they can stop worrying. They have enough to worry about besides me. I push down that anxious knot again.

If I tilt my head to the side, the water stain almost looks like the shape of a person—which makes me remember the shadowy figure and the hand that pushed me down the stairs this afternoon.

And then I'm thinking about ghosts.

As soon as I start, I can't *stop* thinking about ghosts. I keep imagining the hand that shoved me earlier, but now it's grabbing my ankle underneath the blankets or scratching at the glass in the window. I keep imagining that shadowy shape suddenly looming into view over me. I'm pulling from every scary comic I've read and every horror movie I secretly watched at Morgan Clearwater's sleepovers last year even though Mom told me I'm not supposed to watch horror movies.

Probably Mom made that rule for just this reason. I've fed my mind so many creepy stories that it has an endless supply of them to spit back up now.

There's a creaking sound from somewhere downstairs. Mom always tells us it's just the house settling, but right now, it feels more likely that it's a ghost roaming the hallways, making its way up toward us.

I lie there awake for ages thinking about ghosts. The only thing that gets me to *stop* thinking about ghosts is when I start thinking about how I need to use the bathroom instead.

I don't know how late it is—just that it's late. And dark. As I slip out of bed, it's impossible to forget now that I'm walking through what might be a haunted house. The attic doesn't have a bathroom, so I have to creep down the stairs to the second floor. Nanaleen keeps a night-light on the landing, and I can see it glowing through the slightly open door. I skip over the two creakiest steps automatically, just like I've done a thousand times.

The second floor is cold—the whole house is cold, really. The bathroom tiles under my bare feet are freezing. I do my thing and wash my hands as fast as I can, and then I stand there for a long moment, trying to make myself open the door again and go back into the hallway. The prickling feeling on the back of my neck probably isn't from a ghost. It's probably just because I'm *thinking* about ghosts. The hallway will be dark, but not pitch-black—at least there's a night-light. I take a deep breath.

I can do this. I don't have to be brave forever—I just have to be brave for one second.

As soon as I fling open the door and step into the hallway, though, I freeze.

It's not that I see anything, exactly. The dim glow from the night-light doesn't reach the far end of the hallway, and the dark down there seems like a solid thing—like something I could reach out and touch.

Or something that could reach out and touch *me*.

But then I feel it. I can sense it at the end of the hallway. Right where I pointed the camera in that old ghost-hunting video.

Something is . . . *there*.

In books sometimes, people describe their blood

running cold. I've always guessed that was a figure of speech. I've never really thought much about it.

But when I feel the thing at the end of the darkened hallway, that's exactly what happens. My blood runs cold. It starts at the back of my neck, right at the base of my skull, and then it spreads out through my veins like a trickle of freezing water, or like lines of frost splintering out across a windowpane—so slow you can barely trace the movement, until then you can. Everything inside me has turned to ice.

It's the shape from the old video. It's the figure from Nanaleen's photo. It's the thing I sensed outside the closet, and the cold hand that shoved me in the back.

That cold feeling is filling me up now—too big, too overwhelming for me to stop it or hold it inside me. It's growing and growing. I try to push it down, but it only grows bigger. The *thing* is growing bigger, too. I can almost sense it looming toward me, can almost feel it brushing against my skin.

That's where the cold is coming from, I realize. It's coming from this presence. It's like everything this thing touches gets swallowed up into it and turns into ice, or turns into dread. The walls around me are getting darker. The night is closing in. The window at the end of the hall is just a faint black square, like there's nothing at all outside it, and Nanaleen's night-light is barely a speck now. And the thing is still growing. It's still reaching toward me, and I can't push it back.

I run.

I give Nanaleen a silent apology for breaking her no-running rule already, but I don't slow down. I sprint up the stairs two at a time, three at a time, even when I land on the creaky ones. I dive across the room onto my mattress and throw my blankets over myself and lie there with my heart beating fast, fast, fast. Waiting. I can feel my pulse in the lump on my forehead. Any second now, I'm going to feel that thing again. I know it. It's closing in on me, and I can't do anything about it.

But I keep waiting.

And it doesn't come.

It takes a thousand years for my heart to slow down. It takes another thousand for me to finally believe that the thing, the shadowy figure, whatever it is, hasn't followed me. It hasn't swallowed me up into that nothingness.

Not yet.

For hours, I just lie awake and stare at the water stain on the ceiling. The longer I look, the more I start thinking the stain is bigger than the last time we visited. Surely that can't be right—it's only been a few months. Probably I just don't remember how big the spot was in July. Still, I can't shake the feeling that the water stain is growing. I try and try to find new shapes in it—something funny or easy or lighthearted. Something not scary that I can focus on.

Instead, over and over, my mind morphs the brown spot into that growing, shadowy figure.

Why didn't anyone ever repaint this ceiling stain after they fixed the leak in the roof? Why did they just leave this here? Now the spot feels like an omen somehow. It's just a reminder that even though the roof isn't leaking anymore, it did leak once. And it might leak again.

Spotty Signal

I'M EXHAUSTED WHEN MORNING FINALLY COMES. MY EYES FEEL crusty and dry, and my forehead still hurts. In the daylight, it's a little easier to shake the memory of that shadowy figure creeping toward me, but I'm still on edge. I'm still waiting for it to come back.

At breakfast, we dig into the leftover cinnamon rolls from yesterday. Nanaleen says we made enough to feed a small army and we have to help her finish them before we go home. Nanaleen's still in the kitchen waiting on her teakettle when we all settle at the big kitchen table. Rose props a book open under the edge of her plate. Talia has her phone out and is texting again.

I remember what I'd promised myself last night about being cheerful and friendly and happy today, but I'm too tired. I'm spending so much energy just keeping my eyes open that I don't have enough energy left to make jokes and smile and push my grumpiness back where it belongs. I'm frustrated and annoyed at absolutely everything: Talia's phone, and Rose chewing too loud, and the kettle on the stove that's starting to squeal. Even the icing from my cinnamon roll that's stuck to my hands and gluing my fingers together is driving me up a wall.

It's like every bad feeling in me is right up by the surface. It's all right on the edge of spilling over and flooding out into the room around me.

Talia's waving her phone in the air again. "Urghhh," she says.

She waits for one of us to ask what's wrong, which I normally would. But right now I'm too busy trying to scrub the icing off my hands and thinking *urghhh* to deal with Talia's mood.

"Urghhh," Talia says again after neither of us has responded. "I don't have signal again."

"No phones at the table," Rose says without looking up from her book.

"That's a Dad rule, and Dad isn't here."

"Maybe you not having signal is a sign," I tell her. "Maybe the universe is trying to make you follow Dad's rule." Too late, I realize that it didn't come out like the joke I'd meant it to be; it just came out crabby. Talia frowns at me before turning back to her phone.

"I'm pretty sure the universe doesn't care if I'm texting at the table."

"Are you texting Inez again?" Rose asks.

Talia nods. "Mm-hmm. We're gonna meet up at the library later."

I snort before I can stop myself, before I realize how mean it sounds.

"Wow," Talia says. "*Someone* woke up on the wrong side of the bed."

"Everything all right?" Nanaleen asks as she comes over to the table.

She's got her mug clutched in both hands, with the tail of her tea bag and its little yellow label hanging over the side like always. Her skin looks a little paler or more papery again today, and even though her voice is casual, she's looking at me like she already knows everything is *not* all right.

You're not supposed to be making trouble, I remind myself. *You're supposed to be proving that you're happy and fine.* I clamp my mouth shut, and I make myself take a long, slow breath through my nose, which is what Mom always tells us to do when we're feeling mad. It doesn't make the feeling go away. But it lets me bury it deep enough that I can smile over it and act like someone who woke up on the right side of the bed instead.

"Rose and I are going to explore in the basement this morning," I announce, and at least my voice sounds like it's supposed to now. Light and easy and breezy. "Is that okay, Nanaleen?"

Nanaleen sits down at the head of the table and takes a long sip from her mug. "So long as you wear your shoes," she says. "I haven't swept down there in a while. What are you two exploring?"

"We're looking for ghosts," Rose says before I can stop her.

I kick her leg under the table. Rose kicks me right back. Based on the look on her face, she doesn't think she's done anything wrong. I had hoped we could wait to tell Nanaleen anything about our ghost-hunting until we'd found some real proof. Nanaleen might believe in guardian angels, but I don't think she believes in ghosts.

But Nanaleen just says, "Sounds spooky," and she wiggles her fingers in front of her face. It's obvious she thinks we're just playing around like we did a few summers ago. I guess that's okay for now. Maybe it's for the best. "Let me know if you find anything," she adds. "I'd like to know if I've got company here. Maybe I should start charging them rent."

I laugh just so Nanaleen will know I got the joke and look pleased with herself, and then I go back to my cinnamon roll.

"Can we use your old camera again?" Rose asks.

"Sure, if you can find it."

"Or maybe we should go buy a *better* camera."

"Rose." This time, it's Talia who kicks her under

the table—Rose tries to kick back but finds my leg instead, and I jerk. All the dishes on the table rattle. Talia glares at her, but only for a second. She's already turning back to her phone as she adds, "Cameras are expensive."

Nanaleen clears her throat. "I was thinking that we could walk into town this afternoon and get ice cream. Now that the rain's cleared up. The Scooper Dooper's closed up for the season, but Frazer's is still open."

Frazer's doesn't have hand-scooped ice cream cones like the Scooper Dooper does, but Mr. Ben keeps a chest freezer at the front full of ice creams in individual wrappers. It's always stocked with ice-cream sandwiches and Popsicles and Choco Tacos. I study Nanaleen's face, trying to figure out if she's suggesting this because she knows I'm cranky or because she's still worrying over me from yesterday—she knows I can't resist a Choco Taco. There's something off about her this morning, but I can't pinpoint it.

"Yeah," I say carefully, "yeah. That sounds fun."

"Sure," Rose says.

Talia doesn't even look up. "We'll probably still be at the library," she says.

I guess "we" means her and Inez. My cinnamon roll is sticking to my fingers again, and I have to take another deep breath to push the annoyed feeling back down again before it gets any bigger. Up until pretty recently, when Talia said "we," she nearly always meant her and me and Rose.

"We can plan on tomorrow instead, then," Nanaleen says. "Unless your friend wants to join us. She's welcome to. We could swing by the library on our way there."

"That's okay," Talia says.

"All righty," Nanaleen says. "Tomorrow, then." Maybe her smile looks a little more forced today. Or maybe her eyes look more tired. Or maybe there's nothing at all wrong and I'm just imagining it, convincing myself she looks different. I'm probably just on high alert because of the way her smile slipped yesterday. It's like how even though the roof isn't leaking anymore, I can still see the outline of the water stain.

When we start clearing the dishes after breakfast, I wash the icing off my fingers and poke Talia in the shoulder. "You can still help us if you want," I tell her. "With the ghost-hunting. We can wait till you get back."

"Mm," Talia says, and for a second I think she might actually be changing her mind—that she might stay and hang out with us, just like old times, instead of running off with Inez. But she's only paused because her phone is buzzing. She pulls it out to read the text, and then she shoves it back in her pocket.

"That's okay," she tells me, just like she told Nanaleen. "I'm good."

"Okay, cool," I say.

It doesn't feel cool, but it doesn't make a difference either way. I can feel the annoyed, frustrated, bad feeling creeping up in me again. Pushing toward the surface.

And I shove it back down.

Unfinished Basement

NOT ALL BASEMENTS ARE CREEPY. MY PARENTS FIXED UP THE basement of our house in Louisville when I was little. Now Dad keeps his office down there, and Mom moved down the old TV and the giant squashy couch so we can do our Friday movie nights in the basement den. Our neighbor Mrs. Sulaiman has her whole basement carpeted with these thick, plush rugs so soft you want to press your cheek against them, and the basement at Morgan Clearwater's house has at least a dozen beanbags to sit in and also a foosball table. Sure, they might be a little dark and more likely than the rest of the house to have spiders, but I've been in plenty of basements that feel comfy and warm and not at all like some-place you might get murdered.

But Nanaleen's basement is the creepy kind.

Mom and Dad call Nanaleen's basement "unfin-ished," because the floors of it are just bare, cold cement and the walls are just cinder blocks. The elec-trical wires and air ducts that run along the ceiling are all out in the open, all exposed. The basement always feels damp, even though you can't see where any water would be coming from.

I've always thought that calling it "unfinished" is misleading, though, because it sounds like some-body might come along and finish it someday. And at this point, when Nanaleen's basement has been damp and dim and murdery for the last hundred years, I don't think that's going to happen.

Rose makes me go down into the basement first while she waits on the landing. The stairs down here are even steeper than the stairs up to the Dormitory, and the steps don't have backs on them. When I was little, I was always scared that something would reach through the opening and grab my ankles. Maybe I'm still a little scared of that. I'm doing my best not to think about the shadowy figure from last night—which means that of course I'm thinking about the shadowy figure from last night. I keep imagining cold tendrils of that thing inching out through the gaps in the stairs and wrapping around my sneakers.

I have to reach around the corner to find the light switch, but then the lights flicker on, and it's only the basement, with only the normal amount of creepy. There's no shadowy figures in sight—just boxes and boxes lined up along the cement floor. Someone's stapled a couple of curtains up along the back wall's wooden frame, so now that whole end of the basement is just different floral patterns. It was probably Dad. That's just the kind of fixing he does. Maybe he'd decided that curtains would make for cheerier decorations than the exposed wires behind them. The curtains are sagging a little where the staples are coming out, though, and something's nibbled along the bottoms of them.

As soon as I get the lights on, Rose comes

clomping down the stairs after me. I know she packed her regular sneakers for the week, but for some reason, after Nanaleen told us we had to wear shoes down here, Rose decided to put on her big rubber rain boots with the ladybugs on the toes. She's shoved a headband into her hair, but already it's halfway fallen off, and her hair sticks out from under it in five different directions. She looks like one of those obsessed scientists in movies, the kind who yells *Eureka!* a lot and whose experiments might accidentally destroy the world or something.

"Okay," Rose says. She has her hands on her hips as she surveys the stacks and stacks of boxes that fill up Nanaleen's basement. "Where should we start?"

We each pick a corner and get to work opening up boxes. There must be a hundred of them down here—plastic bins held together with duct tape, and moving boxes so old that the cardboard is starting to peel away in layers, and packaging that Nanaleen never got rid of after she ordered cleaning supplies or her waffle iron. Some of the boxes are labeled. Some of them are labeled wrong. I pry open one with big Sharpie letters on its side reading *Shoes (To Donate)*—the box is full of Christmas decorations instead. Then I open a box marked *Christmas Decorations* and find it full of Mom's old art supplies.

"I was hoping we'd just have to find one labeled *Electronics* or something," I say.

"We'll just have to check them all," Rose says. I have to stop myself from groaning. We're going to be down here all day.

Finding the camcorder is our main goal. As we dig through the boxes, Rose starts talking about some book she read at the library a while back about paranormal investigation. Apparently spirits can show up on recordings even when they aren't visible to the normal human eye. I know Rose is still thinking about Talia kicking her after she'd asked about getting a new camera, because she thinks for a while and then says, "Probably the old one is better, anyway."

"Why's that?"

"It uses the big tape things, right? I think the book said it's easier to catch a ghost on a tape than on your phone camera."

"Huh," I say, like that makes sense, and I hope it's not obvious that Rose seems to know way more about all of this stuff than I do. Rose doesn't mean to be a know-it-all, I don't think, but she is anyway. Or maybe it just feels that way because I don't know enough.

When it's time for *Rose* to take the middle school admissions exam, she probably won't be able to flunk even if she tries.

My bad mood from breakfast has turned into a tight, hard knot in the middle of my chest. I imagine strings running out from it and tying around every single one of my muscles, keeping them all tensed up and nervous. I wish Talia were here to help us. It feels weird to be doing stuff without her. Even when Talia and me bicker, we're always together, always egging each other on. When we were in elementary school, we'd walk home together, racing each other from the corner to our front porch every day and keeping a tally of who won. (In the beginning: usually Talia. Once my legs got longer: usually me.) When we played board games as a family, we'd always be on the same team.

But Talia and I don't go to the same school any more, and when we've done family board game nights lately, sometimes she makes plans with her friends instead and then I have to be on a team with Dad. Every morning, I walk to my new middle school that's still only five blocks from our house, and Talia catches the bus to her school on the other side of town.

We're only two years apart in age, but the space between us has started feeling bigger than it used to. I think about her pulling her hand back during our Sibling Conference yesterday. It feels like, lately, Talia's always pulling away.

"...after we find it, right?" Rose is saying, and I realize too late that she's been talking for a while and I haven't been listening at all. I blink at her a couple times.

"Uh...yeah," I say. "Right."

Rose can definitely tell I have no idea what she said, but she just repeats it. "We should plan out what to do next, after we find the camcorder. Right?"

"Right," I echo. "What are you thinking?"

Rose's grin tells me she's just been waiting for me to ask. She pushes her headband farther back onto her head, and it flops forward again right away. "The way I see it," she says, "the first thing we have to figure out is *who*."

I blink at her again, trying to piece together what I'm missing. Maybe I zoned out again. "Who...what?"

"Who's doing the haunting."

"Oh." It hadn't really occurred to me before now, but Rose is right: If there's a ghost in the house— or ghosts—they would probably be the ghost *of* someone. Someone from the past.

"Ghosts usually haunt the place where they died, right?" I say as I pull open another box. It's labeled *M's Good Plates—FRAGILE!* and it does actually look like it holds decorative plates. "Or the place where they lived. So it's probably someone related to us, right?"

Nanaleen's grandfather was the one who built this house over a hundred years ago, and parts of our family have lived here ever since. Generation after generation.

That's a lot of possible ghosts.

"We can look through Nanaleen's photo albums," Rose suggests. "The ones she keeps in the history room."

"And I guess we could go to the library." That gets me thinking about Talia and Inez hanging out there today, but Rose just nods.

"I bet they have old newspapers and yearbooks and things there that might help," she says.

I close up the box of plates and start rummaging through the next one while Rose keeps talking through the plan. My mind has drifted away again, though, to the old family photos Nanaleen keeps on the living room wall. Specifically, I'm thinking about the photo from after Brianna had left. The one where I saw—or thought I saw—the shadowy figure in the background.

Could Brie be haunting Nanaleen's house? Is she even dead? I think all the rest of Nanaleen's siblings have passed away. I remember going to my great-uncle Denny's funeral years ago. I didn't have any dress shoes and so Mom made me wear a hand-me-down pair from Talia that had little flowers cut out around the toes and pinched my feet.

I don't remember meeting a great-aunt Brianna at Uncle Denny's funeral.

"We should find out more about Brie," I say suddenly.

Rose has to move another of the big plastic bins out of the way so she can see me. "Why? You think she's the ghost?"

I do my best to tell her about the photo where Brie was missing, where the shadowy shape had taken her place. Even as I say it, I can imagine Talia rolling her eyes at me, but Rose just shrugs.

"Okay," she says. "That makes as much sense as anything."

I don't know why that makes relief radiate out through me. The strings in my chest and around my muscles loosen a little. "Okay," I say. "Good."

Maybe Brie is the thing I felt in the hallway last night and the hand that pushed me down the stairs — or maybe not. Either way, I feel like something is pulling me to learn more about her. To figure out the story there. Did Brie ever come back to this house after she'd moved away as a teenager? Did she and Nanaleen keep in touch?

Or did she just keep pulling away, until then she was gone?

I've started into the next box, which seems to be mostly full of packing peanuts that aren't padding anything at all, when Rose says, "It's kind of cool, isn't it? The sisters thing."

I stop. "What sisters thing?"

"In the Sisters' Dormitory. How there was Nanaleen and her two sisters, and then Mom and hers, and then me and you and Talia."

"I mean, we're not...," I start, but I don't know how to explain to Rose that I'm not really a *sister* without the conversation turning into something bigger. And it feels like there's bigger things to worry about right now than me trying to explain my gender to my little sister. I crush one of the packing peanuts into little pieces between my fingers and decide to keep it vague. "I don't know if I'd say it like that."

"How would *you* say it?" Rose asks. She hunches over the next box. "I just think it's funny. Three sisters and three sisters and three sisters."

The same spark of annoyance that I felt yesterday during hide-and-seek burns back to life now. *It doesn't matter*, I remind myself. *She doesn't know. It's fine*. But the fire has to go somewhere, and I don't want it to show on my face. I let myself pulverize a whole handful of packing peanuts till they're just little foam crumbs. It's not as satisfying as I want it to be, though, and it doesn't get rid of the annoyed feeling.

It doesn't take us all day to find the camcorder, but it does take us a couple hours. It's close to lunchtime when we finally squeeze open one of the plastic bins and Rose really does shriek, "Eureka!"

The camcorder is nestled right on the top, packed in between wrapped-up cords and a soft-sided camera bag full of extra videotapes. The camcorder is big and clunky, with a foldout screen on one side and a compartment on the other where you can insert the blank tape you're going to record on.

"This thing is a zillion years old," Rose says. "Do you know how to use it?"

"I'll figure it out." I remember the basics, anyway. I try to turn it on, but the little power light stays dark. It probably needs charging.

Farther down in the plastic bin, underneath the camera bag, we find Mom's old Game Boy. It's a brick, with a tiny pixelated screen that's tinted green and doesn't show anything in color. All the buttons on it are huge.

The summer before last, Mom dug out the old Game Boy and let us play around on it. There are only a couple games that still work with it—a baseball game, and some kind of adventure game, and then *Tetris*. That summer, Rose and Talia had gotten bored with it all pretty quickly. But I kind of got hooked on *Tetris*.

I've only just dug out the old game cartridge for it when Nanaleen hollers down the stairs.

"Come on up! Your mom's on the phone!"

"We'll be right there!" Rose yells back, even though I'd be happier staying down in the creepy basement. She starts closing up the boxes we've left open while I pack the camcorder inside its bag.

At the last second before we go upstairs, I shove the old Game Boy and its game cartridge and cord into the pocket of my hoodie.

Mom sounds frazzled on the phone. She must have gone back home for lunch, because I can hear Dad talking in the background, too.

"How's your week going?" Mom asks when it's my turn. "How are you holding up?"

Somehow, I don't think she's just asking about my fall yesterday or the bruise on my head. The knot is back in my chest, tugging on all my muscles at once, tugging on my lungs. Making it a little hard to breathe normally.

"I'm good," I say. I tell the knot to stop, which doesn't work, but I manage to take a deep breath. "I'm doing good."

"What've you been up to?"

For just a second, I think about telling Mom about our ghost-hunting game. I think about telling her how there's something's haunting Nanaleen's house, and how I have a creeping, crawling feeling that something might be wrong with Nanaleen, too. Maybe I could even tell her how *everything's* felt a little wrong lately.

Maybe she would want to know. Dad's perfectly happy to talk about nothing, but it's usually a little bit easier to talk about real stuff with Mom.

"Well...," I start to say.

But then there's a rustling sound on Mom's end. "*Please* don't leave that there."

Her voice is quieter and more muffled than a second ago, like she's holding the phone away from her now. And her tone is suddenly sharper. Sharp enough that I flinch.

"What?" I say.

It's only after she doesn't answer that I figure it

out: She's not talking to me. She must be talking to Dad. I can just barely hear him in the background—I can't make out what he says, just the way that he says it. He answers her, exasperated, and Mom says, "You always do this," and then I can't hear anything else they say because my ears stop working. Instead, my ears start filling up with static, and I'm hovering outside my own body, watching myself, just standing there holding the phone while they fight.

Mom and Dad have always joked around a lot. They used to tease each other and poke fun at each other all the time, always in a way that they both ended up laughing. Like they were in on the joke together.

This isn't friendly, joking-around fighting. It's mad fighting.

"Sorry," Mom says, and her voice is right in the phone again, and just like that I'm slammed back into my own body.

"It's okay," I say. The words come out automatically, though. I feel like I can't catch my breath. "Are you . . . okay?"

"Of course, sweetie," she says. "Everything's okay." There's a pause, and then she says, "It's good to hear your voice. You always brighten my day."

All at once, I'm glad I haven't told her about the ghosts or Nanaleen or anything else. She has enough to worry about. She doesn't need me worrying her on top of everything else.

"You too," I say, and then I add all in a rush, "Rose is here waiting, so I'll talk to you more later. Bye! Love you!"

I hand off the phone to Rose before Mom can say anything. Rose is looking at me a little funny, but she takes the phone anyway and says hello.

There's a hand on my arm. For the quickest second, I think it's the same hand that pushed me down the stairs, but it's just Nanaleen. She touches my shoulder, gently, and I worry she's about to ask me how I'm holding up, too. Or ask me if I'm okay.

But she just says, "What should we have for lunch? Anything you want. We can even do something special. Do you want hamburgers?"

She knows her hamburgers are my favorite. But it's supposed to be just a regular day on a regular visit, and Nanaleen offering to make a special lunch is just reminding me that none of this is regular. I shake my arm out of her grip and give her my most convincing smile.

"We can just do sandwiches," I tell her.

"I know it must be..."

But I don't let her finish that sentence. "Let me know if you want help making them," I say, and then, "I'll be upstairs, okay?"

I head upstairs as fast as I can without technically running. By the time I've made it all the way up to the Dormitory, my side's starting to cramp. But at least my muscles are loosening up a little. I flop down on my mattress and pull the old Game Boy out of my pocket. My whole body loosens a little more. I snap in the game cartridge for *Tetris* and then flip the power switch.

The screen flickers to life.

Falling Blocks

TETRIS IS A PRETTY EASY GAME TO LEARN, BUT IT'S HARD TO get good at. The whole game is just this: different-shaped blocks dropping down the screen while you try to fit them together. When you stack the blocks up without any gaps and get a row perfectly filled in, the row disappears and gives you more space to keep stacking them. I like the way they all fit together like that. I like the feeling when you've got a gap in the row and you don't know how you're going to fix it, and then the right piece comes along and you can slot it perfectly into place.

The summer before last, when Mom first brought

out her old Game Boy, this is what I'd do whenever I was in a bad mood. Or whenever I wanted space from Talia and Rose. Or whenever I just needed my mind to stop running in a million different directions at once. I'd bring the Game Boy upstairs and I'd lie on my bed—or sometimes under my bed so I could plug in the power cord. The outlet is hard to reach from above, and besides, no one would ever have thought to look for me under my own bed. It's the perfect place to be alone.

And then I'd play *Tetris*. The longer you play, the faster the blocks fall, and soon they're dropping so fast that you have to get into this kind of rhythm to keep up. You have to just let your fingers fly across the buttons and let the rest of your brain go quiet. Focusing on just this one thing.

I've gotten really, really good at *Tetris*.

Now, as soon as the game turns on and the familiar music starts up, it's like everything else inside me gets wiped away. I don't have to think about Talia and her friend hanging out at the library without me. I don't have to think about Mom and

Dad arguing. I don't have to think about Nanaleen's slipping smile, or her runaway sister, or the shadowy figure that's haunting the house.

I only have to think about the blocks falling on the screen and finding ways to fit them together. Even when I make a mistake and leave a gap somewhere, I can finish out the row on top of it and get it cleared out, and it's like the mistake never happened. I'm moving, moving, moving without actually having to move at all. Totally in control and totally out of control at the same time.

But for some reason, I can't get my brain to completely shut off the way it used to. Even as I'm playing, my brain's still working in the background. Just a little. It's still thinking about all the things I'm telling myself not to think about, just a little. It's thinking about Mom and Dad in our too-empty house back home. It's thinking about Rose talking over and over about "the sisters thing," and how I didn't have a good way to fix it, out loud *or* in my head. It's thinking about how, if Talia were here, she'd complain about the Game Boy playing the same tune over and over and over again, and I'd probably cave eventually and turn off the volume.

She's not here now. I leave the volume turned all the way up.

But then, right in the middle of the game, right before I can drop a block into place to clear four rows at once and get a *Tetris*—the screen flickers. And then the whole Game Boy shuts itself off.

I should've plugged it in after all, I guess. It's probably run out of batteries. I groan. For the first second or two after it's gone dead, I can still hear the music playing that same tune on a loop, but then it stops. The Dormitory is quiet. Just the hum of air in the furnace vents, and then Rose's voice downstairs on the phone.

And then there's a sound much, much closer to me:

Scritch-scritch-scritch.

I drop the dead Game Boy. It hits my mattress with a *thwump*. I scramble to roll over, to look at the wall beside me, to look for the sound. I make myself stay perfectly still and quiet. I don't breathe.

Scritch-scritch-scritch.

It's coming from inside the wall again, like it was in the history room closet during hide-and-seek. Right beside my head.

Once, a squirrel got inside the chimney of our house in Louisville. Mom was teaching a class and Dad was at work because he hadn't gotten let go from his job yet, and Talia was in charge at home when we heard it scrabbling around inside the fire-place. Talia pretended she wasn't freaked out, but I could tell she was. Rose got so scared she cried. We didn't know what it was at first. We had to call Dad, and he had to call animal control, and when he came home he had to put a big metal trap out-side the fireplace doors and catch the squirrel and drive it out to the other side of the river to let it go.

The *scritch-scritch-scritch*ing inside the Dormi-tory wall doesn't sound exactly like that squirrel scratching around inside our chimney. But it's pretty darn close.

My heart's picked up its pace again, and it feels like someone's walloping a drum inside me. There's a prickling sensation all up my spine. I'm frozen in place. Even though there's no openings in the wall here—no cracks or holes—I keep waiting for a squirrel to burst through it. To come scrambling out of the spot where I'd heard the *scritch*ing.

No, not a squirrel. A rat, maybe. No, not a rat.

A shadowy, growing figure.

My blood's running cold again.

Dad had made us all wait in our bedroom with the door closed while he was catching the squirrel that day. But I got to see it once it was caught. It was weird seeing a squirrel up close like that. It was standing tensed on all four legs inside the cage, tail bunched up, braced to run even though there was nowhere for it to run to. I remember that it was trembling, just a little bit.

Maybe this is an animal inside the wall now, or maybe it's a ghost. But I feel more like *I'm* that squirrel. Hunched and frozen and terrified out of my mind. In the weird, slanting light from the Dormitory window, the water stain over my bed definitely looks like it's growing. Like it's closing in on me.

Just like that thing in the hallway last night.

Dad isn't here now, though, to catch whatever it is. He isn't here to fix this. Mom and Dad have enough on their plates, and I'm not going to give them anything else to deal with.

It's my turn to fix it instead.

I stare at the spot where the *scritch*ing came from, and I take a deep breath. And instead of the anger and frustration that's been here all morning, I try to pull every bit of bravery inside me up to the surface.

We're coming for you, I tell the shadowy figure in my head. *My sisters and I are coming for you. We're going to figure out why you're here, and we're going to stop you.*

I let myself think *sisters*, plural, even though Talia doesn't believe me. Even though she doesn't want to help. The shadowy figure doesn't have to know that. And besides—maybe if I pretend it hard enough, it'll become true. Maybe Talia will stop pulling away.

Maybe I can fix that, too.

The *scritch*ing sound has stopped. The cold, prickling feeling that had been coursing through me fades, dripping away, and it's just me and the Game Boy and the empty Dormitory. I crawl under my bed to plug in the Game Boy's power cord, and then I flip on the switch again. And I let the blocks keep dropping until my brain finally goes quiet.

Late-Night Conversation

WE DON'T DO ANY MORE GHOST-HUNTING THIS AFTERNOON. Talia comes home just in time for supper, and she spends the whole meal telling Nanaleen about some coding project she and Inez started working on together at the library. Of course Talia would spend her fall break doing a coding project *for fun*. And of course Inez couldn't stay her nemesis for long—where else is Talia going to find somebody who's just as thrilled to talk about algorithms or pythons or whatever as she is? It hurts a little for me to admit that when Talia is talking about their project like this, it's the happiest I've seen her in a while. She isn't her usual exasperated or annoyed or embarrassed as she goes on about it—she's just excited.

I can only halfway follow everything she's explaining, though, so I stop listening. I let myself plan out tomorrow's ghost-hunting instead. Rose and I will start out going room by room. Maybe we can find more photos of Brianna that Nanaleen has hung up—or ones *without* Brianna. Maybe we can find another photo where that shadowy thing has taken her place.

There's only one moment when they catch me not paying attention. Nanaleen has to say my name twice, which means I have to fix it to Simon in my head twice as Nanaleen repeats what she said.

"I was thinking we could try for Frazer's tomorrow afternoon if the weather holds up," Nanaleen says. "How's that sound?"

"Sounds good," I say. I don't know if Talia's planning to come with us this time. But Talia's frowning at me like she knows I haven't been listening to her this whole time, so I decide not to ask.

After we head up to bed, and the lights are out,

Talia and I stay up late talking. We've always done this, especially at Nanaleen's house. Back in Louisville, all three of us kids share a bedroom just like we do here, but that bedroom is a lot smaller than the Dormitory. Rose's bed there is only a couple feet away from the bunk bed that Talia and I share, which means it's nearly impossible to talk loud enough that Talia and I can hear each other but quiet enough that Rose can't.

But the Dormitory is perfect for having late-night conversations without keeping Rose awake. Talia's and my beds are tucked along the wall at the very front of the house, and Rose's is clear across the room at the back, beside the stairs. She's sound asleep before we even start talking tonight. I can just barely hear her breathing from this end of the room, quiet and steady.

I like that the late-night conversations are just something for Talia and me. It's not that I don't want to talk with Rose. But at night, it feels like Talia and I can talk about almost anything. It's like we're in a perfect bubble of how things used to be.

Something about the darkness makes it easier to say things, too. You don't have to see the other person's face when you say it, and so it's easier to talk about things that normally you might avoid because you're worrying about how the other person might react. In the dark, you can't see their reaction anyway. In the dark, you can just pretend you're speaking into the void.

That's what I'm pretending when I ask Talia tonight if she knows anything more about Brie.

"She left when Nanaleen was a kid," I tell her, and I repeat back everything Nanaleen told us about her sister yesterday when we were looking at the family photos.

"California, huh?" Talia says when I'm done. "That's already more than I knew."

"Oh," I say, a little disappointed. I'd been hoping that Talia would've picked up something about Brie that someone had told us. Something that I might not have heard, or something I'd forgotten.

"I asked Mom about her once," Talia says. "I don't remember why. Mom had no idea *where* she'd gone. She just said that Brie had moved away, and that I shouldn't pester Nanaleen about her because it would make her sad."

"Oh," I say again.

Talia snorts. "Which is typical, I guess."

I roll over to look at her, even though I can only barely see the shape of her in the dark. "What?"

"Mom and Dad aren't exactly great at talking about things, you know?"

I feel like I should defend them, even though just today I was thinking the same thing. "I mean...," I start, but that's as far as I get. Talia's rustling around on her mattress, maybe rolling over to face right back at me.

"You don't think it's weird?" she says. "How Nanaleen has this sister who just nobody talks about?"

"It kind of makes sense, though," I say. "If Nanaleen doesn't want to talk about it." Nanaleen had seemed okay when I'd been asking her about Brie in the photos, but maybe that's the reason she's seemed so off ever since. Maybe I made her sad by bringing Brie up. Even just imagining it makes me sad, too.

Without really meaning to, I start thinking again about how I'd feel if Talia left like that and then didn't come back home. Did Nanaleen get letters from Brie after she'd left? Did they ever get to talk on the phone? Did she ever hear from her sister again?

If talking about Brie still makes Nanaleen sad, I'm guessing the answer to all those questions is no.

In the ghost movies we watched at Morgan Clearwater's sleepovers, the ghost always had some kind of unfinished business. They were always sticking around because of something left unresolved when they died. If Brie died without ever getting to reconnect with her family...

That sounds like some pretty unfinished business to me.

DUCKLINGS

TALIA DOESN'T COME TO FRAZER'S WITH US THE NEXT DAY AFTER
lunch. By the time Nanaleen is ready to go, Talia
has already walked to town by herself to meet Inez
at the library again. The sun is out today, and the
mist has almost thinned out. It's not that cold, but
Nanaleen makes us put on jackets for the walk anyway. She says it'll get colder as we get closer to the
lake and town. The lakeside is always a little windy,
even in summertime, and I guess in October it can
be brutal.

Rose puts on her big puffy pink coat, and I pull on
my old green jacket over my hoodie. I've still been
wearing my green jacket even though the sleeves

aren't long enough anymore, because I know that when I officially outgrow it, Mom is going to give me the purple jacket Talia outgrew last year instead. Maybe once upon a time I would've been able to ask for a new jacket instead of a hand-me-down, but not now. Not when money is tight. So I'm putting off the change for as long as I can.

Luckily, Mom hasn't noticed my too-short jacket sleeves yet. She's had other things to worry about, I guess.

It's not even that I don't like the purple jacket. I actually really like purple. But I don't like what purple signifies, I guess, or what purple makes other people see: It's like if I wear Talia's hand-me-down purple jacket, everybody is just that much more likely to look at me and think, *Girl*.

I'm Simon, I remind myself now, and I let that warm, glowing feeling swell in my chest for a little while.

The walk into Misty Valley is along the same two-lane highway Dad drove us in on. There's no sidewalk, but there's a pretty wide shoulder, and

Nanaleen always has us walk on the left side of the road so we can see any cars coming.

She's leading the way today, playing a game of I Spy with Rose. I guess technically I'm also playing, but I haven't put in many guesses.

"I spy with my little eye something that is... yellow," Nanaleen says.

"Is it that leaf?" Rose asks, pointing up at a yellow leaf above us. Nanaleen shakes her head. "Is it *that* leaf?" Rose asks. She's pointing at a different leaf now. Nanaleen shakes her head again.

"Is it the sun?" I say before Rose can ask about every single yellow leaf individually.

"Bingo!" Nanaleen says. She stops walking so I can catch up with her, and then she gives me a high five.

"That's not fair," Rose grumbles. "The sun isn't really yellow. It's more like... white. I was reading this book...." She starts telling Nanaleen about how the sun is really all the colors mixed together, which our eyes only know how to interpret as white.

"It's fine," I interrupt her. "You can go next anyway."

"Okay," Rose says. "I spy with my little eye something that's...too small."

She's looking right at me, and so Nanaleen does the same, and Nanaleen's eyes fall on my jacket sleeves where they land a couple inches above my wrists.

"Is it Simon's jacket?" Nanaleen asks.

"Yep!" Rose says with this big grin.

I hunch up my shoulders inside the jacket like that might make my arms shorter, and then I pull on the cuffs. "I don't know what you're talking about," I say.

Nanaleen's still smiling, like she thinks I'm just kidding around. Which I guess is fair. I'd rather she think I'm kidding around than know how my insides have started wriggling like I've swallowed worms. "Looks like it might be time to upgrade," Nanaleen tells me. "We can look through the closet when we get back. I've got heaps of jackets that are just begging to have somebody wear them again."

I tell her okay even though it's not, and then I wait till she and Rose have turned to keep walking and I stick my tongue out at Rose's back.

It's not a long walk into Misty Valley—less than a mile, and mostly flat. But we're not even halfway there when Nanaleen's feet start dragging.

I put off bringing it up. It's the kind of question I don't know if I want an answer to. But soon Nanaleen's trailing a couple feet behind both of us, and when she pauses to catch her breath, I finally ask, "You okay, Nanaleen?"

"To tell you the truth, I might not be up for the walk today," Nanaleen admits. "I'm not as young as I once was."

"Oh," I say. I start to tell her she's still pretty young, but she doesn't look it right now: The lines on her face are deep and gray, and in the afternoon sunshine, her skin looks a little translucent again. She fumbles in her jacket for her pocketbook. That's what Nanaleen always calls her wallet—a pocketbook.

"Here," she says, and she starts pulling out a couple dollar bills. "You two are old enough to go on your own. You can still go get a treat. Tell Mr. Ben I say hi, all right?"

"That's okay," I say too fast. I feel weird about her giving us money, even if it's just for ice cream. I push the bills back into her hand. "We can get ice cream with you another day."

Rose frowns at me. Clearly *she* still wants ice cream today. This is always when I get stuck: when the solution that you know will make one person happy makes another person upset instead.

It only works out okay if the person upset is me.

But Rose is frowning at me now, which makes my insides twist up all over again. I scramble for a way to cheer Rose back up.

"We could go to the library," I tell her. "To do some research. About the...*thing*...we were talking about yesterday."

Rose lights up at that—either because she's happy I remembered her idea from yesterday, or because she's really genuinely excited about doing research about our family history at the library. She's as bad as Talia. "Okay!"

Nanaleen tucks the money back into her

pocketbook, but she looks like she's about to say something else. I cut in before she can.

"We'll go tomorrow," I say again. And then, because I think that Talia would ask it if she were here, I add, "Are you okay, you know, getting home by yourself?"

Nanaleen smiles and pats my cheek with her papery, papery hand. "I'm a grown-up," she assures me. "I think I can manage."

Sometimes, when Rose tries to remind the rest of us of Dad's rules or when I'm trying too hard to fix everything, Mom will tell us, *Let me be the grown-up, please*. As Rose and I head toward town and Nanaleen heads back toward the house, I wish suddenly that Mom and Dad were here. I know I shouldn't. They're dealing with their own things. But it's like a physical wish—this painful tug in my gut.

I push it back down.

❋❋❋

As Rose and I get to the end of the highway and see Main Street up ahead of us, I'm remembering a different day.

Maybe it's a bunch of days all combined together. It seems like something my whole family has done a thousand times. It's an afternoon just like this one, except not like this one at all. It's the middle of summer. I don't have to wear a jacket, and even if I did, the sleeves on my green jacket would still fit my arms. We're walking along the highway into town to get ice cream at the Scooper Dooper. All six of us are there: Mom, Dad, Nanaleen, Talia, Rose, and me, all walking in a line. Nanaleen is humming to herself the way she does sometimes when she's thinking. She isn't slowing down like she did today. Her feet aren't dragging. She looks young still, like someone who could walk for ages without getting tired. Like she always has until now.

Mom is leading the way as we walk, and Dad's bringing up the rear. Dad keeps reminding us kids to stay on the shoulder of the road, even though cars drive pretty slow here because so many families walk along this highway during Misty Valley's summer season.

"Fall in, Bradleys," Dad keeps calling out from the back.

"Do we have to go single file?" Talia complains. "We look like ducklings."

"Quack," Mom tells her from the front of the line, and the rest of us laugh.

We walk like that till we're right on the edge of town, where the path down to the beach starts. The path is along the lakeside instead of beside the road, so Dad lets us break out of line at last and Talia and I take off running. We always race each other down to the little blue shack, just like we always used to race each other from the corner to our house. In the memory, I don't know which of us wins. It isn't really important. The important part is just the running, and Talia and I neck-and-neck, and the warm, glowing, too-big-to-hold-on-to happy feeling that branches out all the way through me.

The whole memory feels like a story that happened to other people, like an old black-and-white photograph. It's easy and smiling and right. It feels like *Tetris* blocks all falling in the right places, fitting together, making perfect rows.

Nowadays, I keep getting the feeling that the blocks are falling too fast, and I don't have time to get them lined up. They just keep stacking up, higher and higher, full of gaps and crooked spaces.

I can't help worrying that they're going to just keep stacking until the whole screen is covered, and there's nowhere left for them to spill over.

YEARBOOKS

ROSE AND I FIND THE MISTY VALLEY PUBLIC LIBRARY EASY
enough on our own. Mom brings us here sometimes
during our summer visits. Usually, as soon as you
step through the front doors, you get smacked in
the face with air-conditioning so cold and refresh-
ing, you have to just stand there in the doorway for
a second to soak it in. This time, I don't think the
air-conditioning is even running. We've gotten to
the weird time of year when the air outside and the
air inside are almost the same temperature.

So the air-conditioning doesn't smack into us.
But Talia nearly does.

It's a close thing. I fly through the library's front

doors without really looking where I'm going, and Talia comes flying toward us from the other direction, and at the last second before we collide, we both yelp and jump backward. Rose is right behind me, and so when I land I stomp hard on her foot, and then Rose yelps, too.

"What're *you* doing here?" Talia asks once we've all gotten our yelps out.

"Change of plans," I say.

"At the library?"

"*You're* at the library," I point out.

"We needed a computer," Talia says, like that's obvious.

"Well, we're doing research," Rose tells her.

Talia's eyebrows go up, and Rose launches into telling her about the old yearbooks and newspapers and our theory that maybe the ghost we're hunting in the old O'Hagan house is actually Nanaleen's sister. Just behind Talia, there's a short girl with glasses and brown skin and a rainbow bandanna tied up around the springy coils of her hair. She's wearing a ripped denim jacket with patches sewn onto the front. I don't want to have to admit that her jacket is cool, but it is.

"Hi, Inez," I say. Inez gives me a little smile and a wave. As annoyed as I am that Talia would rather hang out with Inez than help me and Rose, I guess it isn't really Inez's fault.

"So are you in?" Rose asks as soon as she's finished explaining. "Want to help?"

Right away I wish she hadn't—there's no way Talia will say yes, and so it's just *another* chance for Talia to ditch us. But Inez is perched up on the balls of her feet, looking to Talia.

"That sounds kind of fun?" Inez says, like it's a question.

"You don't have to...," Talia starts, and then she waves a hand at Rose and me kind of vaguely, like we're a bad smell she's trying to fan away. Her face has gone red for some reason—*bright* red. She's the same color she was a couple summers ago when we all spent the day at the lake and Talia didn't listen to Mom's reminders to put on sunscreen. Her face peeled for days after that.

Now, though, this isn't from a sunburn. She's *blushing*. Is she embarrassed by me and Rose? Is this why she doesn't ever let us tag along with her and Inez—because she doesn't want Inez to have to hear us talk about our haunted house theories?

That tense, annoyed knot in my chest is back. It pulls a little tighter.

"Come on!" Rose tells them. "It'll be cool!"

And then Inez shrugs and says, "I'm down," and Talia hesitates for just a second before she reluctantly agrees, and so somehow all four of us end up heading to the back of the library where they keep the old yearbooks and newspapers.

I've never been in this part of the building. Even when Mom used to take us here nearly every day of the summer, we only ever made it as far as the children's section. Mom would pile us all into one of the giant armchairs there and read to us from the books she remembered reading when she was a kid growing up here. Sometimes, she'd find books that were so old, they still had a little index card stuck into a pocket on the back cover. That's how you used to check out books, she told us, before the library got scanners and barcodes.

Mom would show us where she'd written her name in pencil on one of the lines on the cards: *Tessa Walsh*. The first time she showed us, I remember being confused, because now her name is Tessa Bradley. She's got the same last name as Dad and us kids. But Walsh was her maiden name. The old checkout cards only knew Mom from back then, from before she married Dad. They only knew that past version of her.

Sometimes, when my brain goes racing around at night when I'm trying to fall asleep, I start thinking about how my library card in Louisville and my library card in Misty Valley both only know me by my old name, instead of Simon. It's not that there's anything *bad* about my old name—it's just that it isn't me. It's weird to think that the library only knows me as that old, wrong version of me.

It's weird to think that *everybody* only knows me as that old, wrong version. Everybody but me. I didn't think it bothered me, exactly, but now, my throat feels a little tight. There's a little spot of cold in my chest, like an ice chip nestled in too close to my heart.

The local history section has a whole wall of old yearbooks from Misty Valley High School. Talia does some backwards math to figure out the years Nanaleen would have gone there, and then we work out the years for all her brothers and sisters. Rose and I take out the yearbooks from all the years Brie would've been in school, and I spread them out on one of the tables. But Talia and Inez are still at the shelves. Talia's flipping through a yearbook that looks like it's a lot more recent than Brie's.

"You're not going to find anything about the ghost in there," I tell her.

"There is no ghost," Talia says without looking up from the pages. Inez is leaning in close to peek over her shoulder.

I give up for now and focus on our own research. Rose and I split the yearbooks in half and start tracking down Brie's official school pictures from each year. The students are all listed alphabetically, and I start to look under Bradley without really thinking about it, and then under Walsh, because that's Nanaleen's last name now. And then finally I remember that Brie would've had the last name O'Hagan. She lived in the old O'Hagan house back when the house actually held O'Hagans.

And there she is. Brie's face smiles up at us from the page. She would've been a freshman here—probably fourteen or fifteen. Her photo doesn't look much different from the school portraits that Talia, Rose, and I have to take every year, except that it's in black and white.

"She looks kind of like you," Rose says, leaning across the table to see. "Even more in this one."

She slides another book over to me, and there's Brie again. In her freshman photo, her hair was long, but in this next year she's got it cut short, the same way it was in the family photo on Nanaleen's wall. Rose is right—Brie's got almost the same face as me, and with our similar haircuts, it's almost like I'm looking at myself a few years older.

My chest feels warm and light again, even though there's no real reason to be *glad* that I've got things in common with our maybe-ghost.

We line up each yearbook as we find the page with her picture, but when we get to the fourth—the book from what would've been her senior year—she isn't in it. The class photos skip from Richard Ngo straight to Carol Patterson.

It's like Brianna O'Hagan has just disappeared.

"I guess this was when she moved away," Rose says.

"I guess," I say. She hadn't even finished high school, though. Why did Brie leave home?

I study her pictures in the other three yearbooks. In all three of them, she's wearing the same leather jacket—smooth and comfortable-looking, with the collar folded down. The jacket looks familiar, somehow, even though I don't know where I would've seen it before. Even though the photos are kind of grainy, I keep catching myself running a finger over Brie's jacket sleeves like I might feel the texture of it.

"Hey, look who we found," Talia says, and she and Inez plop down at our table. Talia pushes the newer yearbook at me, covering up Brie's class with a different spread of class photos. These are all in color, even though the color is pretty faint. Talia jabs a finger at a photo of a young woman with a big smile and long, shiny, sandy-brown hair.

"Who's that?" I ask.

"Mom," Talia says, like it's obvious. And I guess it is once she's said it.

Mom looks totally different in her old high school photo, and she also looks exactly the same as she does now. I don't understand how both those things can be true, but they are. She's so much younger here, and her smile is so big that it crinkles up her eyes. It's not like Mom doesn't smile nowadays. She smiles a lot. But it's different here, somehow—less tired, more real. Like she's smiling not just for the photo but because she's happy.

The longer I look, though, the more I see how she *hasn't* changed. Her hair in the photo is a little longer, but otherwise it's almost the same as the way she still wears it. Even her glasses here are pretty much the same style she has now, even though I know she must've had to replace them since high school. Probably more than once.

"How old was she here?" Rose asks, and Talia double-checks the year. Mom's last year of high school.

That means Mom and Dad met each other less than a year after this—both of them started college the fall after they graduated. That means this is the version of Mom that Dad first met. Tessa Walsh instead of Tessa Bradley. The same, but not the same. It's weird to think that Mom has had different versions of herself, just like I have. Even weirder when I realize that I have no idea which version is the right one, or the realest one.

For all I know, the version of Mom I know could be old and wrong, too.

Inez has moved on to the other yearbooks we've left open. She's leaning across Talia to skim her finger along the rows of pictures, silently mouthing the names as she reads them.

"So which one is your ghost?" Inez asks.

Talia's face has gone pink again, but she just keeps flipping through Mom's yearbook. I point out Brie's photo for Inez.

"We don't really know if it's her, though," I say. "We don't know very much about her."

Inez starts shuffling through the yearbook's pages. "Guess we should find out whatever we can, then, huh?"

We each take a book and start looking through them. After the class photos, the yearbooks have page after page of photos of different school clubs and sports teams. Then there are a few candid shots from school events. Whenever one of us finds Brie's face, we show it to the group, and slowly, together, we start forming a bigger picture of who she was. Brie was the vice president of her class. Brie was on the basketball team. She started playing the first year Misty Valley High School even *had* a basketball team for girls, and she must've been pretty good. In the book from her junior year, there's a photo of her in her basketball uniform with a big medal around her neck. The caption reads, *Player of the Year: Brianna O'Hagan.*

In that same yearbook, I find a photo of her at a school bake sale. It's the only one we've found so far where she isn't deliberately posed and looking at the camera. This one is candid. She's holding a tray of cookies in one hand, and her other arm is slung around the shoulder of a girl, pulling her close. The girl has a half-eaten cookie and a scrunched-up look on her face, like she just took a bite of it and it isn't very good. She looks like she's laughing with her mouth closed, though. Brie is laughing, too.

As Rose and Inez study the photo, I try to imagine the story here, just like I imagine the stories behind all the photos on Nanaleen's walls. Probably Brie baked these cookies herself for the school sale—baking would've been an inside job, after all. But maybe she wasn't very good at it, and the cookies turned out nasty, and maybe Brie even knew it before she convinced this girl to taste one. Something about the way they're standing makes me feel like they're in on the same private joke, heads close together, totally unaware they're being watched.

Brie looks so relaxed here. It's only now, when we can see her open and free, that I can look at every other photo we've found of her and see how stiff she is. Everywhere else, she looks like she's trying too hard. Like it takes *work* to smile.

But in the photo from the bake sale, she looks...happy. In a wild, overwhelming, all-the-way-to-your-fingertips kind of way.

I know that kind of happy.

It's hard to believe that less than a year after this photo was taken, Brie left Misty Valley and didn't come back. She had her school and her basketball team and this girl, her friend, and she just moved to California. She just left it all behind. Her family, too. Why did she leave them?

It's only later, as me, Talia, and Rose are walking back to Nanaleen's, that the thought hits me: Maybe Brie didn't choose to run away back then. Maybe her parents chose for her. Maybe they kicked her out for some reason.

Maybe she *had* to leave.

Another Late-Night Conversation

ROSE AND I SQUEEZE IN A LITTLE GHOST-HUNTING BEFORE supper. She brings out her unicorn notebook, and I fire up the camcorder, and we work our way through the downstairs rooms: the kitchen, the living room, and the dining room that no one ever uses for dining except on special occasions. Rose keeps writing down the temperatures in each room, but they're not very interesting, and I don't see anything unusual on the camcorder's little flip-out screen. Rose says that if there are spirits around, they might make the film crackle, or they might show up as strange orbs of light.

By the time Nanaleen calls us to eat, we haven't found anything at all. No crackling, no orbs. No shadowy figure at the end of the hallway upstairs.

No Brie.

All afternoon and evening, even as we're hunting for ghosts, my brain keeps running through all the different photos of Brie. Especially the photo of her and her friend at the bake sale. Something about the way they had their arms around each other, so comfortable and easy together, keeps pulling my mind back. It reminds me of how Mom and Dad used to be around each other—how Mom would flick Dad on the back of the head anytime she was passing by, and how Dad would turn around grinning and scoop her into a split-second hug for no reason at all.

I'm still thinking about that photo after we go to bed. I'm still thinking about it while Talia and I stay up late talking.

"Why do you think Brie left?" I ask into the dark.

Talia's quiet for a long while. Sometimes, when she's quiet like this, it's because she's drifted off to sleep right in the middle of our conversation. But then she just says, "I don't know."

"Do you think her parents might have kicked her out?" I ask.

"Honestly, Simon? I don't know. Why would they kick her out?"

"Lots of reasons," I say, even though it's hard to imagine why a parent would kick out their own kid. And this isn't just Brie's parents we're talking about—they're *Nanaleen's* parents. I try to remember everything Nanaleen's told us about her mom and dad, but it's all normal happy family stuff. Big family meals in the dining room downstairs and afternoons at the lake together and that old rolling pin from her mother that Nanaleen still uses. I try to come up with a reason anyway. "Maybe she was a troublemaker. Or maybe she kept skipping school."

"She was vice president of her class," Talia points out, which means that she must've been paying attention to everything we'd found at the library even when she was pretending not to. My mind jumps back to the bake sale photo.

"Maybe she was gay," I say.

I can hear Talia suck in a fast breath. "You think her parents would have kicked her out for being gay?"

"I don't know," I say. "Maybe."

I've read about how sometimes LGBTQ kids get kicked out of their homes if their parents are homophobic or transphobic. It's never been something I've really had to worry about. Even if Mom and Dad knew about my secret name, or my gender, or whatever, I've never worried that they'd throw me out of the house or stop loving me.

"I mean, a lot of people were homophobic back then," I say, trying to get my words in order. "Even more than now. And I just keep thinking about that photo of her with her friend."

"What about it?"

Talia's voice comes out sharp, or maybe it's just the darkness making it seem that way. For once during our late-night conversations, I wish I could see the look on her face to figure out what she's thinking. Then again, maybe I don't wish that.

Maybe, if she's reacting like this, I don't totally want to know what's going on in her head.

All of a sudden this feels like too big a thing to guess at. I backpedal. "I don't know. It's just a guess, you know? I'm just trying to put together the story, but I don't know what—"

"That's right," Talia snaps. "You *don't* know."

She lets out a long breath, like all the air she sucked in a minute ago is leaking back out of her slowly. Like a tire deflating. I watch her, even though it's too dark to see anything. This conversation isn't about me, I know, but it's not *not* about me. Gender and sexuality aren't the same thing, of course— when Mom explained it to us, she said your sexual orientation is who you fall in love with, and your gender is who you *are*—but people who don't fit old society rules for gender *or* sexuality can all be part of the bigger LGBTQ community. *I'm* part of that community. I don't know who I'm going to fall in love with—I haven't even had a crush yet. But I know my gender isn't the one everybody assumed for me when I was born.

I remember that warm feeling I got when Rose and I were looking at Brie's photos, when we realized how much I look like she did. Maybe I like feeling like we're the same in some ways. I like feeling connected with her. Even now, the possibility of it starts warm in my chest, and it keeps spreading through me, warm and glowing—like the feeling I get when I remember I'm Simon.

For the first time, I realize how lucky I am to *know* that Mom and Dad will love me like always no matter what, and that they'll be supportive if I come out to them. How lucky I am to never even have to doubt that.

"Sorry," Talia says finally. I'm surprised at that—both because I didn't really think she was going to talk more with me, and because Talia almost never apologizes. "Sorry for snapping. But...it isn't just a story. It's real people."

I roll over onto my back and stare up at the water stain on the ceiling. "I know that."

The water stain is even bigger than last night. I remember the darkness in the hallway downstairs, and the way it kept growing, creeping outward. The memory is almost enough to push out the warm feeling in me—but not quite.

Just like that, I know: Whoever is haunting Nanaleen's house, it isn't Brie.

It *can't* be Brie. It doesn't feel like her. Maybe Brie really is dead, and maybe she's even a ghost, but she can't be the cold, creeping figure I've been feeling here. I know it deep in my gut. Because whenever I've felt the ghost here—whenever I've felt the shadowy figure—it sends a prickling, creeping feeling through my whole body. The shadowy figure feels like dread.

And whenever I think about my great-aunt Brianna, even with how little we know about her... she makes my insides feel warm. And safe. And maybe a little hopeful.

"Look, I've been wanting to—" Talia starts to say, but then there's a sudden creak from across the room. A jerk of movement.

My heart skips into overdrive. It goes from its normal steady pace to a rapid fluttering in the space of just a second.

It's the shadowy figure.

It's the shadowy figure.

The shadowy figure is here in the Dormitory. Closing in on us.

But when I push myself up onto my elbows to see, it isn't the shadowy figure at all.

It's Rose. Sitting bolt upright in her bed. Staring straight through us in the dark.

Sleep-Talker

"GET IT AWAY," ROSE SAYS.

Her voice sounds wrong, though—it only takes three words for me to hear it. She sounds flat, empty, dead. Her eyes are dead-looking, too, even though I'm pretty sure they're open. It's too dark to see her in much detail, but I can't look away. It's like her empty stare is pulling me in, and pulling in all the air in the room. Pulling in my breath.

Last year, before her chemistry phase, Rose got it into her head that she wanted to be an astronaut when she grows up. She kept telling everybody who would listen about how she wanted to study black holes. The reason black holes are so dark, she said, is because the gravity inside them is so strong that nothing can escape from it—not even light. It had never occurred to me before that that light was something that gravity could affect.

But it is, at least according to Rose. A black hole just keeps pulling and pulling at everything, even light, and not letting any of it go.

"Rose?" I try to say. I can't get enough air, though. My voice comes out a whisper.

Rose just keeps sitting there. Rigid. Staring. The dark feels bigger than it was before, like her eyes are black holes that are pulling in every fragment of light in the room.

Maybe it *is* the shadowy figure after all. Maybe it's already taken Rose, and now it's coming for the rest of us.

"Rose," Talia says, louder. Her voice makes me jump. "Are you awake?"

"I don't want macaroni," Rose says in that same wrong voice.

Just like that, the spell is broken. Talia lets out

a big sigh all at once, like she's breathing the air back into the room.

"She's just talking in her sleep," Talia says.

I wait and wait for my heartbeat to slow down—my brain knows now that it's just Rose, but my body doesn't totally believe it yet. Rose used to talk in her sleep pretty often. She even sleepwalked once or twice. That was ages ago, though, back when she started kindergarten, when she was moody and grumpy all the time about the change in her routine and she never wanted to go to school. Mom and Dad asked our doctor about it back then, and he said it was nothing to worry about. And then, eventually, she stopped doing it.

"Fuzzle Mouth can have my macaroni," Rose says, low and level. It should be funny, but I can't bring myself to laugh.

"Go back to sleep," Talia tells her.

"Okay," Rose says. And then, even though I don't think she ever really *stopped* being asleep, she flops back down against her pillow. Easy as that. Talia lies back down, and I try to do the same, but I can't shake the feeling that there's more to this than just Rose sleep-talking.

Besides, Rose hasn't talked in her sleep in a long, long time.

Talia's quiet for long enough that I think again she might have fallen asleep. When I look over at her bed, though, I can just barely see her eyes. They're open, and for a split second I'm thinking of Rose's empty black hole eyes instead and I have to clamp my fingers around the edge of my quilt, like maybe it can protect me.

"So what were you about to say?" I ask Talia, grabbing onto the only thing I can find as a distraction.

Talia shifts a little. "What?"

"You were saying something. That you've been wanting to..."

"I'm pretty tired," Talia says instead, and then she rolls over in her bed so she's facing the wall instead of me. Her voice comes out muffled into her covers. "We can talk tomorrow. Night, Simon."

"Night," I say. Into the void.

I pull my quilt all the way up to my chin and tell myself over and over to go to sleep. The quilt on my bed is soft cotton, heavy enough that when we visit during the summer, I normally throw it off me in the middle of the night and let it puddle up on the floor. Now I'm glad it's as thick as it is. The warm Simon glow inside me is gone right now, snuffed out like a candle.

The room and the house and everything inside it is cold, cold, cold.

The Jacket

MOM HAS ALWAYS SAID THAT YOUR BRAIN DOES ITS BEST THINKING while you're asleep. I've always figured it was just something she made up to try to get us to go to bed. But there must be some truth to it, I guess, because when I wake up the next morning, I know my brain has been thinking about Brianna. I blink awake, and I look at the long slant of sunlight that's peeking through the Dormitory window, and just like that, I remember where I've seen the jacket Brie was wearing in all her yearbook photos.

I need to get back to my hide-and-seek hiding spot.

Talia's still sound asleep. Rose is sitting up in

bed, though, reading one of her library books. She must hear me tiptoeing across the room, because she looks up from it and waves.

"Morning," she whispers. Her voice and her eyes are totally normal now, but it's hard to shake the memory of them from last night—empty and flat and wrong.

"Morning," I whisper back. And then I ask, "Do you...remember anything from last night?"

She frowns at me, confused. "Remember what?"

I guess that's a no, then. "You talked in your sleep a little," I tell her.

"Oh." She thinks for a minute. "Did I say anything funny?"

"You wanted to give your macaroni to Fuzzle Mouth."

Rose thinks that's hilarious, and I laugh a little, too, trying to act like it was no big deal and like it *didn't* terrify the living daylights out of me at the time. Rose keeps giggling till Talia grumbles at her to be quiet, and I leave her there and creep down the stairs.

I pause on the second floor landing and listen—down in the kitchen, I can hear Nanaleen bumping around, probably cooking breakfast. She's making something that smells sweet and a little buttery—like pancakes, or maybe bread. It's *almost* enough to cover up the stinky-towel smell, but not quite. Now, instead, the whole house just smells like stinky towels *and* whatever Nanaleen is cooking up.

I don't go down to see what it is yet, though. I veer off into the history room. The room is just like I left it after hide-and-seek—with everything that happened after Talia chased me out, I never came back to clean up. The closet doors are hanging open, and the stuffed animals I'd hidden under are exploded everywhere. Fuzzle Mouth is lying facedown beside the doorframe, his legs flopped all the way over onto his head. I pick him up and add him to the pile of other spilled stuffies on the closet floor.

And then I push through the dry cleaning bags and old clothes hanging on the rod above, and I find it.

Brie's jacket.

All her yearbook photos were black and white, but the jacket is a rich brown, like the color of Nanaleen's tea. The leather is just as soft and velvety-smooth as it looked in the pictures. I run my fingers over the folds of the collar, the worn metal buttons, the little scuff in the leather right on the shoulder.

I'm almost positive this jacket belonged to Brie.

Without really thinking about it, I lean my face into the leather and take a deep breath. It smells like something old and woody, like curling up in front of the fireplace on a cold day. In just one breath, it completely pushes out the old-towel smell that's been stuck in my nose for days.

The conviction hits me all over again: Whoever or whatever the shadowy figure is, it isn't the ghost of Brie.

I slide the jacket off the wire hanger Nanaleen's been keeping it on, and I put it on. My arms slide through the sleeves smoothly, like the leather is hugging me. It's a little too big, but it's the kind of thing Mom would say I'd grow into—she's always buying things a little big for us, and especially lately. She says she wants us to get as much wear out of them as we possibly can before we outgrow them. When I got new shoes at the start of this school year, I went from my old sneakers that pinched my toes to new sneakers that are so much longer, I sometimes catch the ends of the toes when I'm climbing stairs and trip.

How old must this jacket be? I try to add it up, but it's too early for math. It's in good shape, though. The buttons and snaps are all still in place, and even though the leather is worn, it doesn't have any holes or anything. Nanaleen has stored it well.

There's a pocket on the jacket's front left side, right over my heart. It's only when I'm fiddling with the button on it that I feel something crinkle and realize there's something inside.

I pull out a little square of paper.

The outside of the note has one letter written in smudgy ink that's faded to a kind of dull blue: *B*. The paper is so old that I'm a little afraid to unfold it—I'm worried I'll rip it. It feels brittle, like the pages in the old books at the university book sale sometimes.

But I just keep staring at that *B*. Is the *B* for *Brianna*?

Suddenly I have that feeling again—the sense that I'm not alone, that I'm being watched. But it doesn't feel like the shadowy figure this time. It doesn't feel cold, or scary. It doesn't feel like dread.

I glance around the history room. There's no one here but me.

Curiosity gets the better of me, and I unfold the paper as carefully as I can and smooth it out on the bed. I had expected a letter or something, but the note inside is short—just six words, all scratched in the same smudgy, faded ink as the *B* on the outside:

> *Meet me in the park.*
> *—Jo*

Beside the name is a drawing of a tiny, scribbly heart.

Jo?

I'm still staring at it, waiting for my brain to catch up, when I notice the smell.

It isn't the old-towel smell anymore. It isn't the tasty breakfast smell from whatever Nanaleen is cooking, either. The smell that's drifting up the stairs is heavy and smoky. Like something burning.

That's when the smoke alarm starts blaring.

BURNTCAKES

I'M ON THE STAIRS BEFORE THE SMOKE ALARM HAS EVEN FINISHED its first beep. When I get to the kitchen, the sound is so loud that I have to clamp my hands over my ears. It feels like it's coming from inside my own brain instead of from the ceiling. It makes it hard to think, and hard to figure out at first where the haze is coming from.

Nanaleen's biggest skillet is perched on the stove, and the burner under it is still on. The blue flames lick up around it. All the air in the room is shimmery and blurry with smoke, but it's blurriest around the skillet—a wide, blackish swirl is rising from the pan. I'm frozen in the doorway, staring at it. Watching it burn.

"Move!" Talia's voice says, and then she's pushing past me into the room. She races to the stove and twists all the knobs all the way to the side to turn them off—then she twists them all again, like she's double-checking. She snatches up a hot pad from the counter—one of the pink-and-orange ones Rose made Nanaleen for Christmas last year, when Rose was in her braiding and weaving phase—and moves the smoking pan off the burner. Then she grabs one of Nanaleen's dish towels.

"Open the windows!" Talia yells over the blaring of the smoke detector.

Rose has joined us here now, and she understands what Talia's doing before I do. She hurries to unlatch the kitchen windows. Everything inside me is panicky and grating, and the smoke alarm makes it all ten times worse. It's making my teeth rattle. Finally, I manage to grab another dish towel and help Talia fan the air, trying to clear the smoke.

"What happened?" Talia calls out. "Are you okay?"

I think for a second that she's talking to me, but she's staring past me, at the open doorway—where

Nanaleen is standing. She has flour dusted on her jeans, and her eyes are wide.

One look at her face tells me Nanaleen is not okay.

Together, we keep fanning the smoke toward the open windows until the air starts to clear. Finally, finally, the alarm goes silent. I slump down against the side of the counter, my bones turning into jelly all at once.

"*At last*," I pant, but my voice sounds strained. My ears are still ringing.

"What happened?" Talia asks Nanaleen again.

Nanaleen comes over to the stove and peers down into the skillet. Her face looks wrong—strange and confused, and she keeps blinking. Maybe it's from the leftover smoke. A little line of it is still trailing from whatever's inside the skillet. I try to take a peek. There are a few circular something-or-others burned onto the bottom of the pan. They look more like hockey pucks or like flattened-out pieces of charcoal than anything you'd want to eat.

"I was...," Nanaleen says. She blinks a couple

more times and tries again. "I was going to make you all pancakes."

"Pancakes," Talia echoes, like she's trying to make the word make sense.

"I wanted to make a big nice breakfast while you're here, since..." She trails off. She's still staring at the burned things in the skillet that used to be pancakes. "I guess I got distracted."

"Distracted." Talia's at a point where she's run out of words of her own, I guess, and can only repeat back whatever Nanaleen says.

"I think you left them on a little too long," I say. I'm trying to make a joke, something offhanded and light to break the tension, but it comes out pretty tense anyway. Everything inside me is still rattling around.

"Did you set a timer?" Talia asks, even though Nanaleen never sets a timer for pancakes. They cook so fast, she's never needed to, and besides, you can tell when they're ready just by looking at them.

Except that it looks like Nanaleen turned on the

stove, poured in the batter, and then walked away and completely forgot about them. "Distracted" doesn't feel like it covers it.

Nanaleen opens and closes her mouth, but she doesn't say anything. Her face looks wrong, like it did the other times this week when her smile slipped. Now, though, she's having a hard time smoothing it back over. She tries to smile but gets stuck. Tries again. Gets stuck again.

Finally, she just repeats, "I was going to make you all pancakes."

Talia sighs, so long and frustrated that Rose and I just stare at her. It's the kind of sigh we're used to her directing at the two of us, but never at a grown-up. Never at Nanaleen.

"You don't have to make us breakfast," Talia says.

"Yeah," I jump in. I'm trying to figure out how to fix all of this, but I feel as useless and burned-out as the used-to-be pancakes. "It's okay. We can have the leftover cinnamon rolls. Or we can have cereal. You have that big box of Frosted Flakes, right?"

"It's fine," Talia says. She doesn't really sound like she thinks it's fine, though.

Nanaleen nods, and she smooths out her blouse, like maybe she can smooth away everything that just happened. "I'll make some tea, then."

She looks around, and her eyes fall on me.

"Brie, want to help me set the table?"

I freeze.

I'd been bracing myself to change the name to Simon in my head—but she doesn't call me by my old name like she usually does. My heart's jumping around. *Brie.* I misheard. I must have misheard.

But Talia is staring at Nanaleen, and then she stares at me. I look down. Too late, I realize I'm still wearing the jacket from the history room closet—*Brie's* jacket. I didn't take it off when I came running downstairs.

Brie.

"I—" I start to say, but Nanaleen's already caught herself.

"Oh, psh—" she says, and her smile slips again for just a second, "—Simon." This time she says it like usual, and I change it like usual. "Help me set the table?"

I feel like I'm outside myself, and I can't make myself move. Talia's still staring.

"Where did you get that jacket?" she asks me.

"I...Upstairs." I feel like I'm in trouble, and I don't know if it's for taking this jacket out, or for confusing Nanaleen somehow, or if I feel anxious and jittery like this just because of everything else that's happening. "I'll...go put it back."

I don't put it back in the history room closet, though. I dash in there to grab the note I'd left spread on the bed, and then I bring both of them up to the Dormitory. I push them under my bed.

When I get back to the kitchen, Rose and Talia are closing the windows back up and putting the dish towels away. Everyone is too quiet, though.

"Well," I say. I swallow. My voice still sounds a little funny. I try to push down the jittery feeling and imagine what Mom or Dad would do if they were here. They always know how to put everybody at ease. They always know the right thing to say.

Except for when they don't, I guess. Then they have to send us away for a whole week just so they can "talk."

I look down at the pancakes in the skillet again. They look more like black Frisbees than pancakes.

"You just made something else instead of pancakes," I blurt out, pointing down at them. "You made burntcakes instead."

Talia's been frowning at Nanaleen all this while, but now she turns the frown on me. "What?"

"Like a Bundt cake, except burnt. Get it?"

Nobody laughs. I can't really blame them. I wish we could go back to ten minutes ago and start this whole day over again. I'm still waiting for Nanaleen to smooth out her face so I can convince myself I only imagined the look on it. But she doesn't.

"Isn't a Bundt cake the kind that's shaped like a big doughnut?" Rose asks.

"Mm-hmm," Nanaleen says, nodding a little.

"This isn't like a Bundt cake at all."

"I know," I say, "but it *sounds* like . . . Never mind."

Talia puts the skillet to soak in the sink, and

we eat cereal and toast for breakfast instead and act like everything's fine. By the time we're settled around the kitchen table with our bowls, Nanaleen looks pretty normal again. I keep having to remind myself to breathe.

It's not until afterward, as the worst of the smoke smell has wafted out the open windows, that I notice the other smell again—the smell of the house this week, musty and sour and bad. The stink from the burntcakes slowly fades away, but the other stink is still there, lingering underneath.

SCRITCH-SCRITCH-SCRITCH

WE DON'T CALL AN OFFICIAL SIBLING CONFERENCE THIS TIME. Instead, while Nanaleen's busy making her second mug of tea, Talia announces that she wants to get some fresh air, and then she gives Rose and me each a look and jerks her head toward the back door. Which means Rose and me apparently want to get some fresh air, too.

It's a little windy out, and by the time we've all three settled in Nanaleen's backyard, my ears have started to ache from the cold. But I'm glad to get out of the house, anyway. More and more, when we're inside the old O'Hagan house, I feel... watched.

Sometimes, the watching doesn't feel so bad—like when I found Brie's jacket. In a way, it's almost comforting to imagine Brie's ghost, or spirit, or whatever might still be in the house, watching over us. *That* does more to make me feel safe than a guardian angel does any day.

But I've been getting that prickling, unsettled feeling more and more, and most of the time, when I feel like something is there...I don't think it's Brie.

Me, Talia, and Rose are all sitting cross-legged in the grass under a trio of tall, tall pine trees. There's one tree apiece for Mom and her two sisters, and they're each just as old as them. Mom told us once that Nanaleen had planted each of these as saplings when each of her daughters was born.

"Okay, so I know you don't believe me about the ghost," I start in, giving Talia my most serious face, "but I don't think it's Brie. Or at least not *just* Brie."

Talia lets out a groan. "Why are you talking about ghosts right now?"

"Isn't that why you brought us out here?"

"No." She's stuffed her hands into her jacket pockets to keep them warm, which makes her shoulders bunch up. "I brought us out here because we need to talk about Nanaleen."

"Because she burned the pancakes?" Rose asks.

"Yes," Talia says. "And no. It's more than that."

"Right," I say. "You're right."

"So what do we do, then?" Talia asks.

Over and over in my mind, I hear Nanaleen say the name: *Brie.* It's not like Nanaleen has never called us the wrong names before. I've been called *Talia* or *Rose* more times than I can count.

But this was different. She'd said it with so much conviction—so sure I was her sister, who she hasn't seen in years. So sure her sister was here.

Because maybe her sister *is* here.

"We should do some more investigating in the house," I say. "I think there might be more than one spirit here, and—"

Talia rounds on me before I even get the sentence out. "Seriously, Simon?"

"What?"

Talia doesn't answer. The wind pushes at us a little harder, and I hunch up my shoulders under my jacket. I'm trying to look her straight in the eye so I can make her understand, but I can tell I'm losing this. I'm losing her.

"I'm going back inside," Talia says, and she shoves herself to her feet. Rose and I stare at each other as she storms back into the house. Something brushes the back of my neck, and I startle, but it's just one of the branches of pine needles. I scoot a few feet away, rubbing the feeling out of my skin.

"Do *you* believe me?" I ask Rose finally.

There's a horrible second when I think she's going to say no. Her eyes are wide, and they keep darting from me to the house's back door where Talia slammed it behind her.

"I think...," Rose starts, but then she pushes her hands into her pockets. "We can do some more researching, if you want. Maybe we can look through the history room?"

When we get back inside, Talia's nowhere to

be found, and Nanaleen has settled in with one of her murder mysteries again. Rose and I start on the second floor this time. It feels good to be *doing* something—even if all we're doing is walking from room to room, videotaping and checking the air temperatures every so often while Rose takes notes.

I'm making a list in my head to go along with the list we wrote in Rose's notebook that first day. The list in my head covers everything that's happened this week that's felt weird or wrong—things that must be related to the haunting, even if I don't understand yet *how* they're related. There are too many things that I don't have another explanation for.

Like: Nanaleen doesn't just forget what she's doing while making pancakes.

And: Nanaleen doesn't burn food. Ever.

And: Nanaleen doesn't lose her place in a recipe she's made a zillion times before.

And: Rose doesn't talk in her sleep. Not anymore. Not in a long time.

I don't know how all of this fits in with the shadowy figure. Maybe the ghost is scrambling our brains. Maybe it's trying to take control, trying to take over.

I just know it all has to be connected somehow. It *feels* true.

When we move into the history room, I close the door behind us. I don't really think that a door will stop the shadowy figure if it's following us, watching us, but it makes me feel better. I try to hold on to that warm, comforted feeling from earlier, when I was trying on Brie's jacket. I'd much rather be closed in here with Brie's spirit than the other one.

Like she's reading my mind, Rose says, "What did you mean about there being more than one ghost?"

I tell her about the shadowy ghost and about how it felt. I try to explain about the feeling I got this morning, too. As I talk, I'm scanning the room with the camcorder, looking for anything unusual. I've got the flip-out screen open again, so it's like I'm seeing double: the miniature, slightly grainy version of the history room that's on the camcorder screen, and then the real version spread out behind it.

"Creepy," Rose says when I'm done. "So you think there's a bad ghost—"

"The one that pushed me," I say, nodding.

"—and then also a good ghost."

"The ghost of Brianna."

Rose crouches down by the shelf where Nanaleen keeps all her photo albums.

"We should check through these, too," Rose says, running her finger along the years marked on each of their spines.

"Good thinking," I say. "Maybe we can find more about—"

But that's when I hear the sound.

Scritch-scritch-scritch.

I lower the camcorder slowly, and I stare at Rose over its screen. She's staring right back up at me. Her eyes are huge and round, just like mine probably are.

"You heard that, right?" I say, and she nods, gnawing on her bottom lip.

Scritch-scritch-scritch.

It's coming from the wall beside Rose, beside the bookshelves. Rose scoots herself back half a step, her eyes fixed on the wall. When I point the camera back at it, there's nothing there. Just my sister and the bookshelf and...

And a dark, tiny gap between the baseboard and the floor. A crack there I've never noticed before.

Something very cold and very slow is creeping up my spine again.

"It's probably nothing, right?" Rose says. "Maybe the house settling?" But she doesn't sound like she really believes it.

I'm holding the camera as steady as I can, aiming it at that gap in the wall. There are two versions I'm seeing again, but this time it's not the version in real life and the version on the camcorder screen. This time, the second version is the one that I'm imagining—the version that *could* happen.

In the first version, the crack stays just the same: small, empty, perfectly still.

In the second version, the crack is growing. It's getting darker and darker, pulling in all the light like a black hole. The gap is growing, looming toward us, the same way I felt the shadowy figure growing the other night, and the cold is spreading all the way through me and taking over and I can't push it down anymore. I can't push it away.

The next *scritch-scritch-scritch* is so loud and so close that I jump back, and the camcorder slips out of my hand.

It crashes to the floor. The fall of it makes the whole room rattle.

Rose screams.

And then something comes out of the wall.

THE MOUSE

AFTERWARD, WHEN NANALEEN GETS THE STORY OUT OF US ONCE she's calmed us down in the kitchen and pressed mugs of hot chocolate into our hands, it sounds like we overreacted.

Rose is the one who tells most of what happened. When we found Nanaleen, it was Rose who finally managed to stop babbling and gasping for long enough to say, "*Mouse!*" Apparently that was a relief for Nanaleen. She'd heard Rose screaming bloody murder, and then heard the racket we were raising as we came thundering downstairs, and I guess Nanaleen thought someone must have died.

"These two get all worked up over a little

mouse," Nanaleen is telling Mom now over the phone. Mom had called right as Nanaleen was getting us settled down at the table. "You'd think they'd never seen one before." Nanaleen laughs a little as she puts it on speakerphone, and then she ruffles my hair. I'm trying hard to play it off like I think it's funny now that it's over, but I'm not doing a very good job. I'm still shaken up. When Nanaleen pats my hair, I jump.

"It was scary!" Rose protests. "All skittery and fast, and its *tail*..." She shudders. "It looked like a wriggly little worm."

"Aren't you planning to be a scientist?" Talia asks, poking her forehead. Talia has a hot chocolate, too, even though she didn't have to go through an ordeal to get it. "Pretty sure scientists can't be so squeamish."

"I'm not going to be a *mouse* scientist," Rose tells her.

Nanaleen shakes her head. "What, you all don't have mice in the city?"

Rose looks horrified. "Not inside our *house*."

"We had mice once," Mom says over the speak-erphone. "When you were a baby, I think." In the background, Dad's voice yells something, and then Mom corrects, "Apparently it was when *Simon* was a baby."

Dad's always been the one to remember all the details about things that happened years ago. Mom used to like it when he cleared up the facts. Now she just sounds annoyed. There's a pause as Dad yells something else.

"He says he remembers because we had to hide all the traps inside cabinets and things, because Simon had just started crawling, and he kept trying to lick them," Mom tells us.

Rose spits out some of her hot chocolate at that, and I make myself laugh again while she and Talia tell me how gross that was, even though I probably wasn't even a year old when I did it.

I'm still replaying that moment in the history room, though. Trying to hold on to every detail so I can make it make sense: The way the room got cold. The way the crack had grown and grown, like the shadows themselves were seeping out from inside the wall. I'd felt that shadowy thing again, the figure, and it had been closer and bigger than ever before.

Even when I saw the mouse come slithering out, my brain couldn't attach the word *mouse* to it till afterward, because it wasn't *just* a mouse. I know it. The mouse I could handle, probably, but the ghost...

It was the ghost at the same time.

Coming out of the very walls. Coming to swallow everything up.

"What do we do now?" Rose is asking Nanaleen. "Do we get a *fu...mi...gator*?" She pronounces it slow, like it's a word she's seen written down before but has never practiced saying out loud. Or like she thinks it's related to an alligator.

"That's for bugs," Talia says. One of our neighbors had to get her house fumigated last year after she got bedbugs. "And besides, fumigators are *really* expensive."

"Do we get an exterminator, then?" Rose asks.

"Those are expensive, too."

"We'll get some traps," Nanaleen says, like that's the end of the matter. And I guess it is. "I'll tell you what: Let's go to Frazer's this afternoon. I'll see if Mr. Ben has mousetraps in stock, and you all can finally get your ice creams."

"Ice cream *and* hot chocolate?" Rose says, eyes lighting up, and Nanaleen laughs.

"That's my job," Nanaleen tells us. "Spoiling you three."

As we're rinsing out our mugs in the sink later, I lean in close to Talia and Rose. "We need to go back for the camcorder," I say in a low voice. "I think I might have recorded it."

Rose's mouth makes a little o. "The ghost?"

"No." Talia slams her mug down in the bottom of the sink, and it sends a wave of cold water sloshing over my hands. "I don't know if you're just really committed to this game, or if you're kidding around, or—"

"I'm not kidding around!"

"Well, with you, it's hard to tell sometimes."

She tells Nanaleen she's going to go into town by herself to meet Inez, and I try not to care. I keep telling myself that Talia will believe me once we've got proof. She'll admit that I was right all along.

But it feels like the cold water from the sink is inside me now instead, filling me up. And I don't have much space left to hold it in.

***

It turns out the camcorder didn't catch anything at all.

I dart in and out of the history room as fast as I can to grab it, and then Rose and I rewatch the footage up in the Dormitory. Rose hovers by my shoulder so she can see the little flip-out screen, and her fingers are clamped on my arm. I'm on edge, eyes straining, waiting for something to appear on the screen as we play it back.

But there's nothing there.

I guess I dropped it at the crucial moment— right before the darkness started seeping out of the wall. One second, Rose is on the little screen, crouching in front of the bookshelf, studying the crack in the wall. And then she yelps, and the camera falls, and I guess the lens cover got snapped shut when it hit the ground because the whole view just goes black. You can still hear screaming, and you can hear our footsteps sprinting away. But then the recording goes on and on, and there's just...nothing.

Slowly, Rose's fingers around my arm loosen as she relaxes. I let out a breath, but I don't feel any more relaxed than I did before we watched it. I'd been scared that we would see a ghost on the camera. Now I'm scared that we didn't.

"What now?" Rose asks. "Should we move on to the next room?"

I feel like a helium balloon that's slowly deflating, letting out more and more air till I'm just a sack of plastic. I know I should be glad that Rose is still on my side—relieved that she's still willing to keep looking for evidence of a haunting here, even though we haven't found much to go on yet.

But I'm just tired. I glance over at my bed and

see the corner of the old Game Boy poking out from under it. I snap the camcorder screen shut.

"Maybe later," I tell Rose.

She looks almost hurt at that for some reason, but then she nods and goes to pick out another of her books. Meanwhile, I settle in on my bed and start up a game of *Tetris*. I try and try to make the blocks fall into the right places until Nanaleen tells us it's time to walk into town.

Frazer's Market

WITH HOW TIRED NANALEEN GOT FROM WALKING THE OTHER DAY, I think we might have to drive into town instead, but Nanaleen insists that she's up for it. The sun has come back out, and it's just warm enough that Nanaleen lets us take off our jackets as we play I Spy along the highway. By the time we get to Frazer's, I've almost convinced myself that everything is back to the way it's supposed to be.

Frazer's Market is cramped and cozy and familiar. All the aisles are just a little bit narrower than you'd expect them to be, and it's hard to walk around inside without bumping into anything. And nothing on the shelves is in order, or at least not in any kind of order I've ever understood. You pretty much have to ask Mr. Ben where to find whatever you're looking for. But if it's something he has in stock, he'll be able to grab it for you right away. *He* knows where things are even if no one else does.

Mr. Ben waves at us when we jingle inside, and he comes out from behind the register to chat. He's wearing a brown-and-white plaid flannel shirt that matches the store's brown-and-white checkerboard floor.

"I'd heard you kids were in town," Mr. Ben says. "Where's your mom and dad?" He turns to Nanaleen. "Did Tessa and Daniel ship the kids off to you this time?"

Nanaleen laughs, and maybe I'm imagining it, but she sounds a little uncomfortable. "This is my grandkid time," she tells him.

Mr. Ben watches Rose and me dig through the chest freezer by the door. "Don't worry, I've still got your Choco Tacos," he tells me. "Got some extra stock in the back, too."

"Oh, right. Thanks." Dad warned me a while back

that they'd stopped making Choco Tacos—which doesn't make any sense, because Choco Tacos are the best. I've been trying not to think about it.

Nanaleen starts telling Mr. Ben about the mouse, and both of them disappear down an aisle to look at the store's selection of mousetraps. When they meet us back at the counter, Nanaleen pays for the mousetraps and our ice creams all at once. I try to see the amount on the cash register, but I can't get a good look.

We settle at one of the little tables Mr. Ben keeps in the back corner, between the soda fountain and the slushy machines—Rose with an ice-cream bar, me with my Choco Taco, and Nanaleen with a huge stack of napkins for the two of us. Which is good, because it's pretty much impossible to eat a Choco Taco without making a giant mess. Right away I start dripping ice cream onto the table. Nanaleen pushes a napkin at me.

What if this is the last Choco Taco I ever get to eat? Why can't anything just stay the same? I try to picture our little group like one of the old black-and-white photographs again. Three people sitting at the table in Frazer's Market, smiling, eating ice cream, making a mess, and cleaning it up. Picture-perfect, like people in a story. I still can't quite imagine it hard enough for it to feel true, but it doesn't *not* feel true. It feels like something that *could* be true, maybe.

"I'm glad we're doing this," Nanaleen says. "I won't pretend I know what it's like, but...I remember when my mom and dad had troubles sometimes. I know it's not easy for you kids."

"It's..." My sentence flickers out, though. All my instincts are telling me to brush her off, to say that it's all fine, that we're fine. I want to tell her that Mom and Dad aren't having "troubles," even though I know Nanaleen probably knows even more about what's going on than I do.

"I don't like it," Rose says simply. She's got a dab of ice cream on her nose. Nanaleen hands her another napkin.

"You know they both love you, right?" Nanaleen says as Rose wipes her face.

"Of course," I hear myself say.

"More than anything. No matter what happens, no matter what they figure out, that's not going to change."

"I know. It'll be fine." I want to be talking about something else. I'm clenching my Choco Taco a little too hard, and too late I realize the shell has cracked. Ice cream starts dripping down my hand in a cold line.

"If you ever want to—" Nanaleen starts, but she's interrupted by the front door of the store jingling again as someone new comes inside. When I peek over my shoulder, I spot Talia and Inez at the front. Talia gives a little wave, and Inez follows her down the aisle toward us, her hands in the pockets of that same cool jean jacket.

Nanaleen waves back at them, and just like that, she's all smiles, and the conversation about Mom and Dad is behind us. I can't say I'm sad about that.

"Glad you found us!" Nanaleen says, like there's any way they could have missed us. Frazer's is usually busy during the summertime, but today Misty

Valley is a ghost town, and it's only us and Mr. Ben here. "This must be Inez. So nice to meet you."

Inez shakes her hand politely. "Thanks for inviting me," she says.

I try to focus on my Choco Taco instead of on the annoyance bubbling up in me that Talia brought Inez. I know it isn't Inez's fault. But it feels like Talia and me are on rockier ground than ever right now, and Inez being here is just another reminder of that. Talia's avoiding my eyes, and her face is bright red again. Why did they even come if she's so worried Rose and me will embarrass her in front of her friend?

But after Nanaleen has gotten their ice creams and they come back to the table, Inez takes the chair beside me. Talia sits down on her other side, eyeing me, but she doesn't seem so frustrated at me anymore. Not like she was back at Nanaleen's house.

"So have you found anything more about your great-aunt yet?" Inez asks me.

I glance at Nanaleen quickly, but Rose has started talking to her about some chemistry experiment she was reading about, and they're not paying any attention to us.

"A little," I say, thinking of the jacket that's still hidden under my bed.

"Have you still been sensing her ghost?"

I think for a second that Inez is making fun of me, but her face is totally serious and waiting, like she's actually interested in what I'm going to say. Talia shifts a little in her seat, but she doesn't say anything.

So just like that, we end up talking about ghosts. I tell Inez about Brie's jacket, and about how I think I might have felt Brie there, but it didn't feel at all like the other ghost we've been tracking. When I describe my theory that maybe the shadowy figure is a second ghost, and that Brie *and* someone else are haunting the old O'Hagan house, Inez nods like it makes sense.

"Maybe Brie's spirit is trying to warn you about the other one," she says, licking some spilled ice cream off her palm.

"Yeah!" I say. "Or maybe she's trying to warn us."

"That too."

Rose has finished her ice cream bar, and she's leaning way forward in her chair now to try to hear us. "What are you guys talking about?"

"Nothing," I tell her. "Just stuff."

Rose glares at me with her mouth pinched up, but Nanaleen is right there listening now, and I'm not about to tell her about ghosts. Not yet, at least.

Something about the way Talia and Inez are sitting now, with their shoulders almost touching and their heads close together, makes me think of the bake sale photo of Brie and her friend. Talia isn't as relaxed or casual as Brie was in that picture, but the closeness between them feels similar, somehow. I keep picturing the other girl in that photo.

Could that be the same person who wrote the note I found in Brie's jacket pocket?

Could the girl from the photo be Jo?

"Simon!"

I don't know how many times Nanaleen has said my name before I'm pulled back out of my own head. She's pushing napkins at me, trying to mop up the puddle of melted ice cream that's pooling under my hands. I didn't even realize I was dripping. I shove the last piece of my Choco Taco into my mouth before it can melt any more, but the melted puddle has reached the edge of the table now, and the ice cream is spilling over and dripping onto Mr. Ben's floor.

"Sorry, sorry," I say as we all try to help clean up the spill. Eventually Mr. Ben has to bring back a mop, and I apologize eighteen times even though he tells me it's not a big deal. Even after it's all cleaned up, my fingers are sticky. I keep clenching and unclenching my hands, like maybe I can wipe the stickiness off on my palms.

For the whole walk home, I'm remembering that puddle of ice cream dripping onto the floor. The shape of it makes me think of the water stain on the Dormitory ceiling, twisted and brownish. Both of them spreading and growing.

The Shadowy Figure

"WHAT DO YOU THINK ABOUT INEZ?" TALIA ASKS ME THAT NIGHT
after we've turned out the lights.

The rain started back up a little after supper,
and now it's pounding on the roof and rattling at
the windows. It's louder in the Dormitory than
anywhere else in the house. Even on days when
it only sprinkles, in the Dormitory, you can hear
every single drop that hits the shingles. Tonight,
the downpour sounds like an army of angry spirits hammering their fists on the roof, trying to get
inside.

If there's any scratching of mice, or ghosts, inside
the walls tonight, I can't hear it. I can't hear much at

all except for the storm and the rain and the thunder echoing off the hills around Misty Valley.

"I like her, I guess," I say, trying to figure out why Talia is asking *me* about Inez. "She seems nice."

Talia's quiet for a long moment. "She is."

"She seems really cool." I let out a snort. "Cooler than you are, anyway."

"Rude," Talia says. But when she talks again, her voice has softened a little. "I like her, too."

"And *she* believes me about the ghosts," I say.

Talia does that long, drawn-out sigh that tells me she's rolling her eyes even though I can't *see* her rolling her eyes. "I think she's just trying to be nice."

"See? She's nicer than you, too."

There's a long pause where I think I might have actually offended Talia. But then she says, "I'm worried about Nanaleen."

It's not where I thought this conversation was going. This is what Talia was trying to talk about in the backyard earlier, but maybe it feels a little easier to have this conversation in the dark. "Worried how?" I ask.

"Worried about her being all alone in this place."

"Because of the ghost?" I say without really thinking about it.

"*No*, Simon. Not because of a ghost. Just because she's . . . You know. Getting older."

I pull at my quilt. "Nanaleen isn't *old*."

"She isn't young."

"She's been living alone in this place for ages, though," I say. I'm staring at the ceiling instead of at Talia, trying to focus on the twisting water stain there instead of focusing too hard on what she's saying. "My whole life. Nearly your whole life." Papaw passed away when Talia was only a baby.

"Right," Talia says. "And she's getting older, and it's too much house to keep up with. I went back into the history room after you all found that mouse—by the looks of it, the mouse you saw isn't the only one here. There were droppings all underneath the bookshelf. I don't think Nanaleen's been in there to clean for a long while."

She's using her grown-up, patient voice as she lays all this out, like the voice Mrs. Ikeda uses in math class when she's trying to explain probability to me for the third time because I still don't understand it. But Mrs. Ikeda is an *actual* grown-up. Talia is only two years older than me.

"Well," I say. My mouth feels a little dry. "We don't know how long those've been there. Maybe the mice are new."

"She's having a harder and harder time with the stairs. Yesterday she wanted something out of storage, and I swear she almost lost her balance trying to get down to the basement."

"But *we're* here now," I say. "*We* can get stuff from the basement for her."

"Right, but we're usually *not* here. That's the whole problem."

Talia's quiet for a long moment, so I'm quiet, too. I want Talia to tell me that everything's okay, or that everything's *going* to be okay, and instead she just keeps talking about everything that's wrong. I don't want to listen to this. Anger is swelling up in me, so fast and sudden it almost catches me off guard. I push it down and push it down, but it's like trying to slam a lid on a volcano. It's not going to be enough.

Stop being mad. Stop being upset.

Lightning flickers outside—the grubby window between our beds goes white for just a moment. I count a full five seconds before the thunder rumbles through, low and ominous.

"I know a while back Mom was talking about taking a couple semesters off from teaching," Talia says finally. "So she could come down here more, to help out. But then Dad lost his job, and so she's the only one making money right now, so..."

"Oh," I say.

Dad's been job hunting for months. It means he can pick Rose up from school, and he's always there when Talia and I get home in the afternoons, but I know that unemployment has been making him restless and twitchy. I'd kind of figured that that was the most important reason for him to hurry up and get hired someplace new—so he'd stop climbing the walls.

I've been trying not to think too hard about the

money part of it. There's too many things to worry about, and somehow, they're all tied together.

When Talia starts talking again, her voice is barely a whisper. It's so quiet it almost gets swallowed by the sound of the rain. "Inez told me that when her parents separated, it started just like this."

"What? No," I blurt out. Too loud to Talia's quiet. Across the room, Rose shifts around but doesn't wake up.

But Talia just whispers, "She said they were stressed about money things, and then a bunch of other little things, and then...Well. They're divorced now."

My insides are all twisted up. I can't decide which part I'm maddest about: that Talia's been telling Inez about our parents, or that Inez thinks her divorced parents are anything at all like Mom and Dad. I stare up at the water stain above me. It's definitely bigger than it was a few days ago. Bigger than it used to be. Maybe the leak in the roof is back. Maybe the rain is seeping through it again, making the water stain worse.

"Does this look bigger to you?" I ask her, pointing my hand up in the dark.

"What?" Talia says.

"This." I show her the water stain. Because of how the ceiling slopes, I can almost touch the spot even when I'm lying down. "Don't you think it's bigger than it used to be?"

"I..." Talia sighs again. "I don't know."

I imagine chipping my fingernail under a corner of the water stain and peeling the whole brownish part off the ceiling and wadding it up into a tiny ball that I can shove into the trash. Bam. Problem solved.

"What if—?" Talia says.

"I think we should add it to the evidence list," I say. I don't realize I've cut her off until I've already done it, and Talia sighs again. I can tell that wherever she'd been angling this conversation, it wasn't here, but I can't stop myself. I can't change direction. "Do you think the ghost could be damaging the house itself? Do you think it could be in the walls?"

"*Simon*," Talia says. "You're not listening to me."

It shouldn't bother me that I have to change

the name in my head. It shouldn't make that pile of anger grow back toward the surface. But something about me having to change the name, combined with Talia saying that I'm not listening, brings it all back up. It takes over me, fast, and it gets stuck in my throat, and suddenly there's a lump there and it feels like everything inside me is about to spill over.

"I—" I start, but now Talia cuts me off.

"Good night," she says, her voice prickly and sharp, and she lies back down away from me. Facing the wall. I squint my eyes shut against the dark and tell myself not to cry. There's no reason to cry. I don't know why I'm upset. There's no good reason to be upset.

But knowing that doesn't make it stop, and the bad feeling in me is growing, growing, growing, no matter how hard I try to hold it back.

I'm remembering that day when I looked up the meaning of my secret name, when I learned that Simon means "listen." I've wanted so badly to fit into that name—or for the name to fit me. I've told myself it's something I can become, even if I'm not already. Because I *want* to be Simon, because being Simon makes me feel happy.

But I'm not happy right now. And I'm not good at listening. And it's starting to feel like I never will be.

You're not listening to me.

The angry, cold feeling is too big inside me now, even though I know Talia doesn't know about my secret name and doesn't know about its meaning. I tell myself over and over that it doesn't matter, that there's no good reason to be upset, but I'm spiraling, and I'm moving too fast, and I'm out of control. I've got the same feeling I had when I was running down the hallway the other day during hide-and-seek. I'm sliding in my socks, too much momentum to change direction anymore.

Even if I'm heading for a crash.

✷✷✷

I don't know how late it is when I finally fall asleep, but it's late. And I don't know how late it is when I wake up again. But it's even later—so late that it's probably early.

And the shadowy figure is in the room. It's right in front of me.

For the first time, I don't just feel it. It's not just a shape in a photograph. I don't need a camcorder and screen to pick it up.

I *see* it.

My blood runs cold.

I sit bolt upright in the dark. The rain has stopped. The house is quiet except for my own breathing, fast and shallow. Every other sound is swallowed by the figure in the middle of the room, a growing, terrifying outline of a shape that's creeping outward like billowing smoke, or like a black hole.

My pulse is in my ears, beating like a drum. It takes everything in me to tear my eyes away from the figure, but I do, just long enough to look over at Talia's bed. She's a lump under the covers, sound asleep.

I look over at Rose's bed across the room.

Rose isn't there.

Static goes through my brain, sharp and

crackling. Panic. A bad, bad thought is creeping up my spine: that maybe the figure has already swallowed up the rest of the house. That it's been growing and growing until it's swallowed up everything around us. Everything I know.

And now it's taken Rose.

The shape is still getting bigger, inching toward me. I can't see it growing, exactly, but I can tell. It's like my brain keeps rewriting the second before, filling in the missing gaps as the shadow gets bigger and bigger and closer and closer. It's pulling at me, and pulling, and pulling, and there's a scream inside me that's getting pulled closer and closer to the surface.

Run, I think, but there's nowhere to run—the shadowy figure is filling almost the entire room now. *Hide*, I think, but there's nowhere to hide, either. *Be brave*, I tell myself, but I'm filled with panic instead, and I don't have enough brave left in me for this—not even one second of brave.

"Let her go," I whisper, but it's like my voice gets swallowed by the shadow.

It's already swallowed up Rose, and it's proba-bly swallowed Nanaleen, and it's going to take Talia and then me. It's too much to push back. I start to close my eyes, like that can put off the inevitable.

At the last second, though, just before I can close them, my eyes fall on a streak of soft brown on the floor. The sleeve of Brie's jacket. It's dan-gling out from where I shoved the jacket under my bed.

I remember what Inez had said, that maybe Brie was trying to warn us. Or protect us. I reach for the jacket, and I clutch the sleeve of it, my fingers tight around the soft leather.

Brie, I think desperately, uselessly. *Help us.*

And the shadowy figure is gone.

Just like that.

I open my eyes. The room is still pitch-dark, but it's the normal dark of nighttime now. My heart's still pounding, but there's nothing there. Just me, sitting up stock-still in my bed. And Talia, still asleep. And . . .

"Brie?" I whisper into the dark.

There's no response. Everything is quiet. I let the jacket flop back onto the floor, replaying the moment in my mind when I asked her for help and the thing disappeared. The hairs on the back of my neck prickle.

When I look over at Rose's bed again, though, it's still empty.

That's enough to get me on my feet.

I keep expecting the shadowy figure to reappear, to take back over the whole room, but it doesn't. It's gone, or hidden, at least for now. But Rose is gone. Did it take her? Did it take Nanaleen?

There's a creaking sound from downstairs.

My heart's pounding as I tiptoe across the room, the floorboards freezing under my bare feet. Rose's covers are tossed aside, and her blanket is draped on the floor. I peer down to the bottom of the stairs. The door is ajar, and the faint light from the hallway night-light makes it into an outline. I creep down the stairs, slowly, skipping the two creakiest steps.

At the bottom, I make myself reach for the door

handle. I'm waiting for the shadowy figure to reappear at any second now. I'm waiting to fling open this door and find only darkness and cold—to find that the shadow has already swallowed up the whole rest of the world.

But the door jerks open before I can touch it.

There's a girl.

She's barely more than an outline. Her hair is tossed and wild, like it got caught in a huge wind. Her eyes are wide, and she's screaming, or maybe *I'm* screaming.

"*Shhh!*" Rose hisses, and she clamps a clammy hand over my mouth.

It takes a long second for my brain to understand. *It's Rose. It's just Rose.* I stop screaming, but the sound still rings in the night, lingering in my ears like the blaring of the smoke detector. There's too much panic in me, and even the relief that Rose is here, that she didn't get taken by the shadowy figure, isn't enough to make it stop. I try and try to breathe.

Rose still has her hand over my mouth, so I lick

her palm and make her move. She squeaks and wipes her hand on her pajamas.

"What are you doing down here?" she whispers.

"What are *you* doing?" I demand.

"I was..." She shakes her head. "I must've been sleepwalking. I woke up down here. I was just going back to bed."

My mind makes up an image of Rose wandering the hallway down here, drifting along, her eyes totally blank and empty. I remember that scary, flat voice she used when she was talking in her sleep last night.

Empty. Empty. Empty.

I don't know how to say all that, though, so instead I just say, "You haven't sleepwalked for a long time."

"I know," she says. Her mouth twists over to one side like she's about to go on, but she doesn't. She just shrugs.

We go back up the stairs. One at a time, single file, like our own line of ducklings. Rose goes back to her bed. I go back to mine. My heart hasn't slowed down, though, and the static in my mind is still there. The water stain over my bed has grown huge and yawning. It's nearly as big as I am. I imagine it sagging toward me, closer and closer.

Pulling me in till there's nothing left.

I roll over instead to look at Brie's jacket still hanging out from under my bed. I remember that moment when I'd asked her for help in my mind. When I'd thought of Brie, and the shadowy figure had disappeared, just like that.

Thank you, I think at her, even though I don't know if I can feel her here anymore. I feel like I'm fraying, tugging loose from all the walls like those curtains Dad stapled up in the unfinished basement.

It's the unknown that's getting to me. I'm scrambling for answers.

But as I stare down at that jacket, I realize there's one person who might be able to give me answers. Who might know about the shadowy figure—and know how to make it stop.

We need to talk to Brie.

ACTION ITEM

"WE SHOULD HOLD A SÉANCE."

Rose and Talia both just stare at me after I say it. We're all back up in the Dormitory after breakfast the next morning. I tried to call an official Sibling Conference to present my idea, but Talia said she was in a hurry to go over to Inez's house and could we please just skip the ceremony. Which means this isn't really a Sibling Conference, I guess. It's just talking with my siblings.

But Talia and Rose both stare at me for so long without saying anything that it's barely even that.

"Well?" I say. "Did you hear me?"

"We heard you," Talia says. "I'm just waiting for you to tell us that you're joking."

"What's a séance?" Rose asks.

"It's a ghost-summoning. I think. Like when you try to contact spirits. You light candles, and you invite the ghosts to come speak with you, and then you get them to communicate with you with a talking board or blinking lights or something."

"Ohhh, a *see*-ants," Rose says. "I've read about those." She pronounces it just like that: *see*-ants. I guess that's what happens when you've only ever read the word in a book.

"And I'm not joking," I tell Talia. "We need answers. And I think there's someone here who has them. We need to talk to Brie."

"That's an absolutely terrible idea," Talia says.

"Why?" I demand.

"Well, it could be dangerous, for one."

"*Brie* isn't dangerous," I tell her. "I think Brie is one of the ghosts here, but she's not the one I'm worried about." I tell them about last night—about the shadowy figure that appeared right here in the Dormitory, and how when I asked Brie for help, it vanished.

Talia rubs her forehead. "Simon..."

"Besides, I thought you didn't even believe in ghosts," I point out. "If ghosts aren't real, what's the danger?"

This whole time, Talia's been alternating between looking at the two of us and looking down at her phone. Probably she's texting Inez about why she's running late, explaining that her younger siblings are acting silly or immature. The thought makes another wave of hot, angry frustration push through me. The feeling's been growing all night, getting bigger and bigger like a gathering storm.

Now, though, Talia finally slides her phone back into her pocket. She focuses her frown on me and only me.

"I don't think there's a *danger*, exactly," she says in that annoying grown-up voice. "But I still don't think you should go messing around trying to summon spirits."

"We're not 'messing around.' We're trying to find answers. If we can just talk to Brie—"

"You know what I mean. And besides, it won't work, and then you're going to be...You know. Disappointed."

Another surge of anger. "You don't know it won't work."

"I don't think this is really about ghosts," Talia says. She hasn't turned away from us yet, but she's stepping backward toward the staircase already, a hand out behind her so she can catch the railing.

"What else would it be about?" I demand.

But Talia just pushes onward like she hasn't heard me. "And I don't really want to deal with you after you have to admit this isn't really about ghosts."

She's right at the top of the stairs now. For just one horrible second, I imagine the shadowy figure shoving her down them, just like I got shoved the other day. I imagine the look of shock that would flash on her face. I imagine her tumbling head over heels. *She'll* have *to accept ghosts are real now*, I think.

The satisfaction from that thought flares and then puffs out right away, though. Guilt comes afterward. It twists and tangles up with the anger that's still inside me. I'm talking before I can stop myself.

"Look, if you don't want to help us, fine," I say. "Just stay out of our way."

Talia *does* get that look of shock on her face now. Just for a moment. Her eyes go wide, and then they go dull and blank. Empty. She spins and stomps down the stairs without another word. The door at the bottom gets stuck for a second when she tries to slam it shut, but she slams it again. And then again. On the third try, it finally sticks.

Rose and I look at each other.

She must be able to see how angry I am, even now. It's rolling off me in waves. I try to push it back down, to make myself smile and pretend everything's fine, but I can't. It's too big and too much.

"So when do you want to do the séance?" Rose asks finally.

She says it like there's *two* questions in there: the one she's asking out loud, and then a second one underneath, asking, *Do you still want to do the séance?* She pronounces *séance* right this time, though, slowly and carefully, trying it out.

I still want to do the séance. I *need* to do the séance. I need to be doing something, solving something, making some kind of progress toward lining up the pieces at last.

Even if this isn't an official Sibling Conference, I need an action item.

So I make one for myself. "Tonight," I tell Rose. "I'll figure out what we need and get everything together. And then we'll do it tonight."

✳✳✳

Rose suggests that we do some more filming today, but I'm not in the mood. Catching the ghost on film isn't going to solve this. It's not enough anymore. I need time to think. Or, even better—I need to *stop* thinking for a while.

So instead of ghost-hunting, I plug Mom's old Game Boy back into the outlet under my bed upstairs. I wriggle myself underneath the bed frame, and I hold the Game Boy just close enough to the edge where the light still hits so that I can see the screen.

And then I spend the whole morning playing *Tetris*.

For hours, I get sucked into the game completely—pulled in so it's just my fingers flying on the buttons and the only thing I can think about is where to slide the next block into place. I set a new high score. Then I play another round and beat *that* high score with an even higher one. I drop a piece wrong, and then another, and for a second it looks like it's all going to spiral out of control, but then the right piece appears at just the right time and I can fill in the gaps perfectly.

It's almost enough to settle me back into myself, to stop the twisting, anxious feeling that's been burning through me.

Almost.

There's exactly one thing I don't like about *Tetris*, or at least the version of *Tetris* I play on Mom's Game Boy: You never really *win*. Even when you get a high score, you're always going to lose in the end. That's the only way the game ever finishes. No matter how many points you've gotten, no matter how many close escapes you've managed when you've saved yourself and fixed it all at the last second—the game always ends with you eventually running out of space. When you do, the speaker plays this jarring buzzing sound, and it blocks out the whole screen in an instant. *GAME OVER* blinks up at you.

It doesn't matter how well you play or for how long. It's just how the game works. Always, eventually, you're going to run out of options and crash.

Walking in Circles

BY THE AFTERNOON, EVEN *TETRIS* CAN'T KEEP MY BRAIN QUIET. I'm bouncing out of my own skin, and I can hardly wait till the séance tonight. I need to get out of the house, but it's too cold to be outside without having something to do.

"Can I help with anything outside?" I ask Nanaleen. "Maybe I could haul branches?" The rainstorm dropped a lot of tree branches around Nanaleen's house into the yard. I remember a couple summers ago, when we had a storm like this, and Nanaleen got our cousins Ethan and Owen to pull all the fallen branches back to the burn pile and cut them small enough to burn. They got to use her huge pruning shears, which look like giant scissors you have to hold with both hands.

Nanaleen looks confused at first, like she's surprised I *want* to help. "You could help me wash the windows," she suggests.

I don't know how to explain to her that I need to get out of this house. "Could I rake, maybe?"

Nanaleen shakes her head. "There's a boy in town who helps me with all that," she tells me.

Oh, right, I think dully. Hauling branches or raking leaves are both outside jobs. Washing windows is an inside job. It surges up in me again, that frustration, that feeling like I'm never going to actually get to be Simon to anybody except me. The anger is always in me now, right under the surface, and it's getting harder and harder to pretend it isn't. It's getting harder to keep acting like everything's okay.

I guess some of the not-okay is showing on my face, because Nanaleen backtracks. "Maybe we need a break from being cooped up in here," she says. "Should we go for a walk?"

It's as good an excuse as any to get out of here.

Nanaleen invites Rose along with us, and I worry for a second that Rose might agree to come, but she's settled down in front of the TV, watching another of her nature shows. Nanaleen promises her that we'll just be in the yard if she needs anything. By the frustrated look on Rose's face, I guess it must be a bummer of a show. Although maybe her frowning isn't from the TV at all.

Nanaleen's yard is filled with flower beds and vegetable beds and tidy little paths she's laid out of stones. Even now, when the flowers and vegetables are brownish and dead for the winter, the whole yard is meticulous. At the edge of the yard, where the vegetable garden ends, everything orderly that she's put in around the house suddenly stops, and then it turns into the woods, which are thick and dense and overgrown. Definitely *dis*orderly. It's like the old O'Hagan house sits in a little pocket of tidiness with wilderness pressed in on all sides.

Nanaleen used to keep a few paths cleared so we could walk in the woods without worrying about poison ivy, but they're overgrown now. We stick to walking slow circles around the main yard instead. I try not to think about what Talia said last night, about this being too much house for Nanaleen to keep up with by herself.

We take it slow, stopping to check on different plants that have withered for the season but should come back next year. When we've looped around to the three big pine trees in the back, Nanaleen looks up at them, her hands folded behind her back.

"It makes me so happy to see how you three kids get along," she says.

I must be making a face at that, because she laughs. "I don't mean you don't bicker. But you all love each other. *And* you like each other. That's special. It seems like you all really enjoy spending time together."

"Talia doesn't," I say before I can stop myself.

Nanaleen gives me a hard look. "She's a teenager. She's figuring out who she is and what she wants. But I think she's glad to have you and Rose, still."

I try to make myself believe that. Nanaleen had twice as many siblings as me, after all. Maybe she's right.

As we're passing the front of the house, I look all the way up to the little square of window between Talia's and my beds in the Dormitory. Brie's jacket is still wadded up under my bed there. Suddenly I remember the note I found in the pocket of it.

Maybe Nanaleen would know who Jo was. Maybe she can tell me what happened to Brie, and why she left. After what Talia told me the other night, I haven't wanted to ask Nanaleen anything else about her sister—I haven't wanted to make her sad. But we're talking about siblings now, and I don't see a better time. If Nanaleen doesn't want to tell me about Brie, she'll say so.

But I start to ask the question at last, and then I freeze.

And I can't do it.

Not because I don't know if Nanaleen can handle it. Because I don't know if *I* can handle it. I feel like I'm getting to know Brianna, even just through the little pieces of her history that we've found. The more I learn about her, the closer to her I feel.

But I don't know how her story turned out. And it's the kind of question I'm a little afraid to know the answer to.

We've walked partway down the driveway when one of Nanaleen's neighbors drives past in her pickup truck. She pulls over onto the shoulder of the empty highway and rolls down her window to say hi.

"That was some storm we had last night, huh?" the neighbor says, and she and Nanaleen chat for a couple minutes about the weather and church and how the neighbor's daughter's stationery business is doing. It takes a while for the neighbor to notice me, and then she smiles really big, like she thinks I'm five years old instead of nearly twelve.

"And who do we have here?" she asks Nanaleen. "Is this your grandson?"

I've been bracing myself to fix in my head whatever she's about to say, but then she says it and I blink.

I don't have to change it at all. She actually said "grandson."

The jumping feeling in my stomach settles for the first time all day. Even as Nanaleen corrects her, even as Nanaleen introduces her with my other name, I tune them out and try to hold on to just that one word: *grandson*. I try to let the warm, glowing feeling fill me up again, right to my fingertips.

✳✳✳

When the neighbor drives off, Nanaleen and I head back toward the house. We stop on the front porch, knocking mud off the bottoms of our shoes.

"I know it's maybe not what you'd planned," Nanaleen says, "but I sure am glad you all got to come visit this week."

"I'm glad, too," I tell her.

And I'm not even just saying it because I know it's what she wants to hear. I really mean it. Even with the ghosts and everything that's been wrong or off this week, I'm glad we're here.

The Séance

I SPEND THE REST OF THE AFTERNOON GETTING READY FOR OUR séance. I borrow Nanaleen's computer to do a little research about how we should prepare, skimming articles and videos until I have a pretty good sense of what materials we'll need. Some of the sources suggest different things, and some of them have suggestions that I don't have time to track down by tonight—like a psychic medium, or a Ouija board. But over and over, they all emphasize that the most important part of the whole ritual is your intention. You have to believe in what you're doing. You have to know what you intend to find.

That won't be a problem, then. I know exactly

who we need to talk to: Brie. We need to ask her what she knows about the shadowy ghost, and we need to get her help getting rid of it. We need her to help us fix everything.

I have a whole lot of intention.

I wait until Rose and Nanaleen have settled in the dining room to play an afternoon round of Parcheesi, and then I creep into the kitchen to gather up supplies: candles, matches, a bunch of dried herbs from her spice cabinet, and the little blue ceramic bowl she always uses to melt butter. One of Nanaleen's guardian angel statues is perched on a shelf above the sink. It watches me as I rummage around and shove everything into a plastic grocery sack.

Last, I take down the old family photo from the living room wall. It's the most recent one of Brie that Nanaleen has hanging up—the last one from before she left. I tuck it into my bag, too, and race upstairs to hide it all under my bed.

And now we just have to wait until nightfall.

I've been trying to work out where Rose and I

should try to do the séance, but the answer lands right in my lap at suppertime, when Nanaleen tells us that Talia called and asked to stay the night at Inez's house. She's going to watch a movie with Inez's family, I guess. Nanaleen looks right at me as she says it, and I know she's thinking about our conversation earlier. For just a split second, my insides clench up. Talia's pulling away.

But Talia being out of the way means Rose and I can hold our séance in the Dormitory. Which is the best possible place here to hold a séance for Brie. It's the Sisters' Dormitory, after all. This is the same bedroom where Nanaleen and her sisters grew up—which means it's the room where Brie lived. Of all the rooms in Nanaleen's house, this one should have the strongest connection to her.

After we go to bed, Rose and I both pretend to sleep until we can hear Nanaleen turning in for the night. I'm wide awake, though, and humming with energy. I can hardly lie still. The *scritch-scritch-scritch* sound has started up again, which means the mousetraps Nanaleen put out yesterday haven't done their job yet—or that the sound isn't just a mouse. It feels like it's coming from all around me now, closing in. The water stain over my bed is the biggest it's ever been.

We hear Nanaleen's door close, which means she's gone to bed. I make myself count to a hundred to make sure she isn't getting up again. The house is quiet, though.

It's time.

It's not until I pour out my plastic bag and fold Brie's jacket in the middle of the floor that it all starts to feel very real.

Rose brings over her flashlight, and her eyes are wide and anxious in its dim beam. I know she's feeling it, too—the prickling feeling now that something is about to *happen*. I pour the herbs into the chipped blue bowl, and Rose sets up the candles, and we prepare our space just like the articles I read said to. We fold Brie's jacket in the middle of what will be our circle, and then we place the frame with Brie's picture—the whole family's picture—up on top of it.

"Did you think to bring matches?" Rose whispers.

We're whispering even though I don't think Nanaleen could hear us from up here, even if she were still awake. We're whispering because it feels like a night for whispering.

"Of course," I whisper back. But when I pull out the matchbox, both of us realize we don't know how to light a match. I've seen people do it plenty of times, but when Rose and I take turns trying, neither of us can get more than a little spark.

After I flick one match so hard that the head of it goes shooting off into the far corner of the Dormitory, Rose slides the matchbox shut.

"Do we *really* need candles?" she says.

"I guess not," I say, even though it feels like a bad way to start. But we already avoided one fire this week, and I don't really want to risk starting another one.

The most important part is the intention, I remind myself. I close my eyes for a second and imagine myself pulling all my intention up to the surface. I imagine it filling me up.

We sit down cross-legged on the floor, just

like we do for our Sibling Conferences. Our circle doesn't feel complete with just two of us, but neither of us says so. The bowl of herbs, the jacket, and the old black-and-white photograph are on the floor between us. Brie's face smiles up at me. Pointed and short-haired and so much like my own.

"Okay," I say.

"Okay," Rose says.

We both take each other's hands, and then we close our eyes.

In the dark behind my eyelids, everything that's been happening this week feels far away. The whole house feels distant, like we're not really there. We could be anywhere or nowhere. When I talk, my voice sounds different. It's like our old ghost-hunting videos from two years ago, when we were pretending to be Dr. Skeffington and Rose Raven. My voice is too close and loud, but also removed, like it isn't really mine.

"Brie," I hear myself say. "Brianna O'Hagan. If you're there, we want to talk to you. Please. We need your help. We need to know what you've been trying to say."

Quiet.

And then cold.

It sneaks up on me, that prickling, icy feeling that creeps up my back. My eyes snap open. First I just feel it, and then I see it—that shadowy figure, closing in around us.

Rose's breathing is shaky, but it's not until I squeeze her hands that she opens her eyes, too. She looks up. I wait for the second when I'll see it in her eyes—when she sees the ghost.

But the second doesn't come. She just looks at me, a question on her face.

"What?" she whispers.

The shadows are all around us, filling me up, and I want her to see them—I want her to see it too and admit that I've been right, and then help me figure out what to do. Help me fix this. But she doesn't see anything, and I'm clenching her hands too hard, and the shadowy figure is wrapping us up, and everything's cold.

"*What?*" Rose whispers again, more urgent.

Brie, I think. *We need you.*

I take a long breath. Focus my intention. My thoughts are running in twelve different directions, and my body wants to run, too, wants to get away from everything that's closing in on us, but I pull it all in and try to be brave, just for one more minute. I try to focus everything inside me on just this one thing.

"Brie?" I whisper.

The shadowy figure has stopped growing. It's just there, just shadows, and as I stare across our makeshift circle at my sister, I can almost believe that the darkness is just normal darkness. That the cold is just normal cold. Rose's hands are clenched tight around mine now, too, tensed and ready, like the deer with their little white tails. But she's just responding to *my* panic. She's not panicking herself.

"Brie?" I say again. Not a whisper this time. I let it come out a little louder.

I wait for something to happen. Time is moving weirdly—I can't tell how much of it is passing. I squint my eyes shut, and I wait, and I wait.

I make myself count to ten, slow.

When I open my eyes, the shadowy figure isn't even there. It's just us in the room.

In *Tetris*, there's always a moment when you realize you're done for. When the blocks are falling too fast and you can't get them into place. When you make a mistake at one crucial moment and know you won't be able to fix it this time.

That moment feels just like this. Like the waiting that we're doing now, waiting for something to happen and slowly realizing it isn't going to. Except that when that feeling is happening during *Tetris*, you're at least still scrambling to save it. You're at least doing *something*.

"Maybe we need to tell her *how* to communicate," I say finally. "We could ask her to make a noise. Knock her knuckles on the floor. Or..." My mind's running wild again. My eyes fall on Rose's necklace, the one she's always chewing on. "Here, we can use a pendulum." One of the articles online suggested letting a pendulum dangle on its string and asking the ghost to move it.

Rose unclasps her necklace and hands it over,

but her face is pinched. Her mouth has pulled tight, like she's holding back on saying what she's really thinking. The intention in me is seeping away slowly, sliding through my fingers like sand. Something else is replacing it. A bad feeling. But it isn't like the shadowy figure—not anymore. It's angry and frustrated and just...bad.

I hold the necklace out in front of me, letting the pendant on the bottom of it dangle free.

"Brie," I start again. The more that bad feeling fills me, the harder it is to keep my voice steady, but I push the feeling down. "Show us that you're here. Give us a sign."

I'm staring so hard at the pendant that my eyes are watering. I'm afraid to blink. Afraid I'll miss the moment when it moves. For a split second I trick myself into believing that it's shifting, quivering in the air—but it's just me. *I'm* moving. My hand is clutched so tight around the necklace chain that the pendant has started to shake.

"Here, you hold it," I tell Rose, shoving it at her. "You've got steadier hands."

Rose doesn't hold it up, though. "Simon," she starts.

"Hold it still," I say.

Rose's face pinches even tighter. But she takes the necklace from me. She holds it still.

We both watch it. I make myself count to twenty. Fifty. A hundred.

The pendulum moves a little. But it's only because Rose's hand starts to drop.

"Hold it still!" I say again. I'm nowhere close to whispering anymore. I'm talking so loud that I might wake Nanaleen up. I don't even care. I'm getting frustrated, and I'm running out of energy to hide it.

But Rose doesn't put the necklace back up. She wads the chain up into her palm instead and clenches her fist around it tight.

"Simon," she starts again, "I don't think it's working."

"Because you're not holding it right," I say.

I reach for the necklace again, but she doesn't hand it over. Her chin is trembling a little bit. Like she's about to cry. That just makes me madder.

"It's probably because you couldn't get the can-dles lit," I'm saying, with that bad, angry feeling growing inside me, even though *I* couldn't get the candles lit, either. "Or because you aren't focusing right. You have to have *intention*. You have to *want* it to work."

Rose's face has gone red and splotchy from try-ing not to cry, but I can already tell her eyes are wet. "I *wanted* to find evidence," she says shakily. "But we tried, and..."

"No," I say. "No. We just have to keep trying. We'll figure it out."

"Do you think...maybe...Talia was right?" Rose says.

The blocks are falling too fast.

I don't decide to stand up—I just suddenly am standing. The anger inside me is too big now. It's too much. It's spilling out of me, and I can't hold it in, and I don't *want* to hold it in. If I don't let it out, I'll explode.

I'm clenching my fists so tight that my finger-nails cut into my palms. But it's not enough—not enough to get the anger out, or to turn it into something that can fit inside me. I kick the floor. Hard. I'm not wearing shoes, and my toes slam into the floorboards so hard they feel like they might break. It still isn't enough, though.

There's too much there. It's like every bad feeling I've ever pushed down is spilling out of me now, overflowing.

Rose is staring at me. Her eyes are huge and watery. I feel like *I* might start crying, too, just as a way to get all of this out. All this *feeling*. To push the too-big anger out of me.

Okay, I *am* crying now. My throat is clenched up tight and tears are pushing out of me, but it still isn't enough.

The bowl of herbs is still on the floor.

I kick it, hard.

It goes flying at the wall. Rose yelps. I kicked it with the inside of my foot, the way I learned to kick during soccer, the way you can give your kick more control, but I don't feel in control at all now. And I don't even *play* soccer anymore, because soccer changed from something fun and easy into something I had to fix in my head, just like everything else, and it turned into a place where I had to make a choice I wasn't ready to make and deal with things I didn't want to deal with yet, and so I quit. And I've pretended it was fine, and I've pretended everything is fine, and I've kept pushing down every bad feeling until now. Until I can't anymore. Until it's all spilling over.

The chipped blue bowl hits the wall, hard, and breaks. And just like that, something in me breaks, too.

The anger's gone. All kicked out of me. But it's like the anger had grown so much that it had already pushed everything else out of me, and so once it's gone, I'm left with . . . nothing.

I'm just empty.

Rose and I are both just standing there, staring at the broken bowl. I'm breathing hard, but otherwise, everything is quiet. I wait for Nanaleen to come upstairs. Surely she heard the crash. Surely she'll come up to see what's going on.

But the house is quiet. If Nanaleen heard us, she's not going to do anything about it. It's like Talia said, I guess. Nanaleen's been having a harder and harder time climbing the stairs.

The broken pieces of the old blue bowl are lying in a pile of spilled basil and thyme and cinnamon.

"I think Talia was right," Rose says finally. It isn't a question this time. I don't have anything left in me to feel now—I can't even be mad at her for saying it. Not when I know it's probably true. "I think . . . maybe this isn't really about ghosts."

"What else would it be about?" I hear myself saying.

She doesn't answer.

But she doesn't have to, I guess. My mind's already racing in a thousand different directions. Answering my own question, if I'm ready to listen.

Spilling Over

MOM ALWAYS TELLS ME I HAVE A VERY ACTIVE IMAGINATION. SHE says I imagine things so hard, I make them true in my mind.

Sometimes she's right.

Rose and I don't talk as we pick up the broken pieces of the bowl as carefully as we can. We don't talk as we put the unlit candles and candleholders back into the bag. We don't talk as we slide the old family photograph into the bag, too, and shove all of it out of the way against the wall.

We leave the spilled herbs there on the floor to deal with tomorrow.

Rose goes back to bed. I go back to bed.

But I don't go to sleep.

I lie there and stare at the water stain on the ceiling and I try not to think. My mind is running through the list of evidence, though—all the things we wrote on the list in Rose's notebook, and all the things we didn't. The water stain really is bigger than it used to be. I'm sure about it now. The stretch of brown is longer than ever, and it's making the drywall sag a little.

But now, with everything pushed out of me, I can hear what Talia was trying to say. The water stain is real, and it really is a problem that needs to be fixed and repaired. But it isn't evidence of ghosts.

I sit up fast. There's too much in my head, and I need a way to focus it. To make it go quiet. Rose has already fallen asleep, I guess, because she doesn't stir when I get out of bed. She doesn't move at all as I wriggle myself underneath my bed and feel in the dark for the outlet there. I plug in the old Game Boy.

I make sure that the volume on it is turned all

the way down before I hit the power switch, and then I roll all the way under the bed, with my hands and the Game Boy close enough to the edge that there's just enough light to see the screen. And I start up a new game of *Tetris*.

I don't want to think. Not right now.

But as the blocks on the screen start to fall, as I try to line them up, my brain doesn't shut down. It just keeps moving faster, even as the game gets faster right along with it. I run through the list of evidence, and over and over, I realize how it's not evidence at all. Not of ghosts, anyway. I've been taking it and jumping to conclusions instead of listening—changing it, growing it, making it fit into the story I wanted instead of the story that was really happening.

It's not that I *wanted* the ghost to be real, exactly.

But a ghost is simpler, in some ways. It's easier to face than all the complicated pieces that have been changing all around me.

The scratching I've been hearing in the walls,

the mice—it just means Nanaleen's house is getting older, that maybe it's too big of a place for her to live in all by herself anymore. The bad, musty smell—it's not from a haunting. It's just water and age. The water that's been leaking under the roof up here all week might not be the worst of it—there might be more water damage, more leaks that need to be looked at.

It's easier to just pretend they're not there, or to blame it all on something ghostly and supernatural.

Even the other day when I knew, I *knew* that a hand pushed me on those stairs... Now that I'm realizing how much else of this story I've been making up, forcing into place, I'm realizing how I might have tricked myself. How I imagined it so hard that it became true. Because even now, if I think hard enough about it, I can *almost* feel a hand pushing my back. I can *almost* make myself believe it.

But there's nothing there. It's just me, trying to make a different answer than the one Talia's been trying to tell me.

Lying here on my stomach, I can see clear

across the room. I can see the spices all spilled out from our séance. I can see Brie's jacket tumbled on the floor, a brown pile of leather that, if you didn't know what it was, wouldn't look like anything. It's deflated and sad.

Maybe it was easier to think about Brie's story than my own.

And maybe it was easier to play our ghost-hunting game than think about everything else. It gave me just one thing to focus on.

The blocks in the game are falling faster than ever. I can't keep up. I can't get them to fit together. I run out of space, and even with the volume turned all the way down and no buzzing sound when it happens, I jump when the screen flickers away. *GAME OVER.*

I wanted to be able to fix everything—all the things that have been wrong, all the things that have been changing. Mom and Dad. Nanaleen. Talia. Rose. I wanted it all to be something I could put back and make into a perfect story, like an old black-and-white photograph from the past.

But maybe even the old photographs aren't as perfect as I might wish.

You're not listening to me, Simon.

Talia's known all along that this wasn't really about ghosts, I think. But I haven't wanted to listen to her talk about what it's really been about—so I haven't. I haven't listened at all.

I start another *Tetris* round. This time I lose it even faster. *GAME OVER.* Start again. *GAME OVER.* I can't get any of it stacked where I want it. I can't get any of it right. I can't make it fit together.

And no matter how hard I try to make my brain stop going, it doesn't work. It just keeps running and running.

Early-Morning Conversation

AS MY BRAIN KEEPS JUMPING AROUND AND REFUSING TO TURN off, I try to do the one thing that always, always makes me happy. The thing that reminds me what happy even feels like.

I remind myself that I'm Simon.

I'm a boy and my name is Simon, I think, and it's true. I know it's true. The warm feeling is there in my chest.

But it's all mixed up with that prickling feeling I've started getting when, over and over, I have to fix my name in my head. I haven't told them anything else, because I've figured it was easier that way, and so I know it isn't their fault that they're calling me the wrong name and I know I shouldn't feel annoyed.

But I do. And maybe I should be listening to that, too.

I don't *have* to tell anyone my secret name or my pronouns.

I don't *have* to come out to anyone at all. Not now, not ever, not if I'm not ready or don't want to. It's my journey and my choice. Only mine.

Whatever I choose, I can find a way to be happy.

But I lie there under my bed and realize that I haven't even been *letting* myself choose. I just decided that there were too many other things to worry about, and I didn't want to be one of them. I decided that with so many other things changing, it just wasn't the right time to tell my family about this other change, too. About me.

I figured they were happier not knowing.

So instead I've let *myself* be unhappy.

I don't know how long I'm awake under the bed. Finally, I give up on stopping my brain from spiraling, and instead I just let it go. I let it spiral and spiral until it's spiraled itself out. Until I'm tired and empty and just done. It doesn't fix anything. There's no mystery to unravel or problem to solve with one easy solution.

So I just try to breathe, until finally the breathing gets easier, just a little bit.

✳✳✳

In the early morning, I hear the footsteps.

I'm still underneath my bed. I must have fallen asleep at last. My cheek is pressed against the Game Boy's buttons, and when I blink my eyes open, I realize that it's still turned on. *GAME OVER*, the screen says.

More footsteps. Closer this time.

I blink again, and then Talia is there.

She's crouched beside my bed, holding up the corner of my quilt, her head tipped sideways to see me underneath. She's just a silhouette at first, an empty outline surrounded by the pale daylight from the window behind her. But then my eyes adjust, and I can see her face better.

"Hey, Simon," she says.

"Hey," I say.

My voice sounds rusty and raw, but Talia doesn't comment on it. She doesn't comment on my face, either, even though it's probably red and puffy. It's always red and puffy after I cry. Even the next morning. Rose's face will probably be red and puffy this morning, too.

Talia just crouches there for a long time, and then, without warning, she flops down on the floor on her stomach. And then she wriggles in after me.

I have to scoot myself over a little so she can fit under the bed with me. I make sure the Game Boy is finally switched off, and I push it to the side to make room.

And then Talia just waits.

We're both quiet for a while, but I always get tired of the quiet before Talia does. That's probably what she's counting on. She doesn't even have to ask what I'm doing down here, because she knows she can just wait me out.

"I'm okay," I say finally.

Talia nods. "Yep. Sure. That's why you've been on the floor under your bed all night."

"I haven't been here *all* night."

"Right," she says, like she's remembering. "You and Rose did your séance."

She doesn't have to ask how it went. Maybe she'll bring it up again later to rub it in about how she's been right all along—but probably not. Talia's never been really big on *I told you so*'s.

"You're back early," I say.

"Yeah," she says. "Inez wakes up, like, *annoyingly* early. Crack of dawn, apparently. Her family invited me to stick around for breakfast, but..." She shrugs, which is probably hard considering she's lying on her stomach under my bed. But it's enough of a shrug that I get the meaning. "I wanted to be back here."

"Oh," I say.

"Rose is still asleep, I think."

"Oh," I say again.

We're quiet for a while longer. Quiet like we are during our late-night conversations sometimes, when I think that maybe Talia's fallen asleep. But she's awake now. We both are. I can see her gnawing on her lip, thinking about something.

"Sorry that I've been kind of brushing you off this week," she says finally.

I don't realize until after she's said it that that's all I've really been needing. I just needed her to acknowledge it, I guess. To show that it wasn't just something I imagined. That I'm not the only one who's noticed everything changing.

"It's okay," I say. "Sorry I've been kind of a pest about it."

"Hmm," she says. "Part of being siblings, I guess."

She says "siblings" instead of "sisters." I don't think that she does it on purpose, or probably even realizes she's done it at all. She still doesn't know about my secret name yet. But there it is anyway: "siblings," not "sisters." I don't even have to fix it in my head.

I prop my chin up on my hands so the top of my head brushes the bottom of the bed frame.

"It's fine that you want to hang out with Inez instead of us," I say. "*Without* us. I get it. You're allowed to have friends besides me and Rose." I tip my head her way and let myself grin a little bit. It's not forced and on-purpose like it has been for a lot of this week. This smile feels like it's just kind of slipped out. "Even though me and Rose will always be the best," I add.

Talia props her chin on her own hands and smiles, a mirror to me. "You two aren't getting rid of me," she assures me.

"I know."

We're quiet for a while longer. Talia's fidgeting with her hands a little now—the way *I* do sometimes, the way she always tells me to stop doing. She fidgets and fidgets, and then something resolves on her face.

"Inez *is* my friend," she says at last. She lets out a long breath through her fingers. "But she's also...kind of...my girlfriend?"

I whirl toward her so fast that I whack the top of my head on the bed frame, and my hair gets tangled in the slats on the underside of it. And then, as I'm trying to get *un*tangled, I kind of elbow Talia in the face, and she yelps and rolls backward to avoid getting hit in the nose.

"Sorry, sorry!" I say. "Wait, go back. You said it like it's a question. *Kind of* your girlfriend?"

Talia groans and buries her face in her arms. Her face has gone pink. Even after she's hidden it, I can see the pink around her ears. But I don't think she's embarrassed, not totally. I think she's happy, too.

"Okay, yes," she says into her own elbow. "She's my girlfriend. She kissed me at the end of our visit this summer, right before we went home, and I didn't know what to do, and then we texted about it, and then I found out she was going to be here for fall break, too, and..." She buries her face even deeper. "We talked about it last night. Made it official."

"That's awesome!" I say.

Talia peeks up at me. "Really?"

"Yeah! She seems really nice. And you both like the same boring stuff, like robots."

Talia punches me in the arm, and when I try to jump out of the way, I get tangled in the bed frame again. Thank goodness I cut my hair short, or else I'd *really* be in trouble down here.

"I didn't know if she liked girls for a long while," Talia says. "I didn't know if *I* liked girls."

"But yes, and yes, right?" I say.

Her face goes even pinker, but she's smiling. "Yeah."

I realize suddenly that we're talking about this during the daylight. Talking about *real* things. Even though we're wedged underneath my bed, there's enough light to see each other's faces. We can see how the other person is reacting, and it's okay. We can still talk about things.

"I'm really happy for you," I say, and I mean it.

"When you brought it up the other night, about Nanaleen's sister and how she might have been gay..." Talia shakes her head, but it's not at me. "I almost told you then."

"Huh," I say. I try to replay the conversation from that night in my mind.

"For a second there, I thought that maybe you already knew, even. I thought..."

I'd been trying to read her in the dark that night, I guess, but I wasn't really ready to listen to whatever *she'd* been thinking about. I was too caught up in my own thing.

I'm going to do better, I decide. *I'm going to listen better.*

"I didn't really leave you an opening," I say finally. "Sorry. I'm glad you told me now."

"Me too."

"She does seem really cool," I say. "I liked hanging out with her."

"I've been trying to keep her away from you," Talia says. "You and Rose both. I was worried that you'd...You know. Figure it out."

I remember how red her face went when we ran into her and Inez at the library. And here I'd thought she was embarrassed by *us*.

"That's why you never used to let us hang out with you?" I say, incredulous, and Talia laughs.

"Yeah. I figured if anyone was going to realize I

had a crush on her, it would be you two. You know me better than anyone."

It's that moment in *Tetris* when you think a block is going to land wrong, but then at the last second, you slide it right into place. The knot that's been so tight in my chest is starting to loosen a little. I can breathe. I keep breathing.

There's a shuffling sound from beside the bed, another rustle of footsteps. And then Rose's face pops down in front of us.

"Oh, hey," she says, like it's totally normal to find her two older siblings lying underneath the bed in the morning. But then her eyes narrow a little. "Wait. Are y'all having a Sibling Conference?"

"Not officially," Talia says.

"Not without the third member," I add. "That's against the rules."

I wriggle myself farther under the bed, all the way up against the wall, and Talia wriggles herself in the other direction, and then she pats the floor in between us. Rose's face lights up. She flops down on the floor and starts wedging herself into the space. It's kind of a tangle to fit us all down here, and Rose manages to kick both of us more than once. But the whole time, I'm thinking about the way I yelled at Rose last night, and about how all this time, she's been by my side, trying to help me. Even when she didn't know how. Even when I didn't want her to.

I've been brushing her off this week just like Talia's been brushing *me* off.

"Hey," I tell her, and I poke her in the shoulder until she looks at me. "You did a good job with the research this week. I should've said that earlier. A *lot* of times earlier."

Rose watches me for a second, like she's making sure I'm being sincere. Then she grins. "Well, yeah," she says. "I'm a good scientist."

"You should probably be the head of the research team," I tell her. "If we ever have to do this ghost-hunting thing again."

"We are *not* doing this ghost-hunting thing again," Talia says.

"You didn't even do it this time!" Rose points out.

"*If* we have to investigate another haunting," I say, "I nominate Rose Raven to be in charge."

Rose glows at that.

All this while I've worried that Talia was pulling away from me. I didn't even realize that Rose was worrying that *I* was pulling away from *her*, too.

None of us are pulling away from each other now, though. We don't have space to. We're packed in under the bed like sardines, or like well-placed *Tetris* blocks. Or like we will be in the back seat later today when we ride back home with Mom and Dad.

Talia must be reading my thoughts, because she says, "Guess we'll see Mom and Dad later today."

"Yeah," I say.

Rose doesn't respond at first. She hasn't brushed her hair this morning, and it's sticking up all over the place, like she's a scientist who got into a fight with static electricity and lost. A piece of it is stuck under the mattress already. Talia reaches up and tries to pull it free.

"Are Mom and Dad splitting up?" Rose asks suddenly.

Talia lets her hand drop. "Why do you ask that?"

"Why are you *not* asking that?" Rose says. "Haven't you noticed how weird they've both been?"

"*I've* noticed," Talia says. "I just didn't know *you* had...." She shakes her head.

"Are they getting a divorce?" Rose asks.

"What?" I blurt out. "No."

"No," Talia agrees, and the knot inside me loosens a little. But then she says, "Not yet, I don't think."

I wanted it to be something I could solve or fix. I really, really wanted that.

"Do you think they're going to?" I ask after a minute.

Talia lets out a long breath through her teeth. "I don't know. I don't know what's going to happen."

"Have they talked with you at all?" Rose asks her. "About what's going on between them?"

"No." Talia snorts. "Of course not. They haven't said *anything*'s going on between them. When I've tried to ask, Mom's been all, 'We're fine! Everything's fine!' Even though clearly they're *not* fine, and we all know they're tense with each other. But they'll just go on for as long as they can, I guess, pretending nothing's wrong."

"Until they can't anymore," I say. "Until it all spills over."

I think about the ghosts I've imagined all week— every bad feeling I've pushed down, growing inside me until it overflows. I've been trying so hard to pretend that everything was fine—like if I could just pretend it hard enough, it would become true. But that doesn't work for everything. It doesn't work for this.

Talia is studying my face. "You're angry," she says.

"No, I'm not," I say. But I am. It's there just under the surface, spiraling out from my chest all over again. I'm angry at Mom and Dad, even though I don't know what I'm angry about.

"Yes, you are," Talia says. She reaches across Rose to poke my shoulder. "You're angry. And that's fine. You're allowed to have feelings, you know."

"Yeah," Rose chimes in. "You don't have to pretend to be happy all the time."

"I'm not pretending," I say automatically. But I guess I have been, a little. Based on the faces Talia and Rose are making, they both know it. "Okay, I'm not *always* pretending."

Talia's still making that face. She waits.

"I'm fine, mostly," I insist.

"You're still doing it," Rose points out. "You're doing the exact same thing as Mom and Dad."

I groan and bury my face in my arms. "I just don't want to bother anybody," I say with my voice muffled in my elbow. "Or worry anybody."

There's a shuffling sound, and then Talia's finger is jabbing me hard on the top of my head. "Maybe we *want* to be bothered," she says. "It's not like you're going to scare us off. We like you, you know? We *want* to know when you're not okay."

I guess I've never thought about it like that. And I guess I wouldn't want Talia or Rose to hide it from me when *they're* struggling.

It's part of being siblings. I'd want to know. I'd want to be there.

When I unbury my face, they're both starting

to smile, and we all lie there together for a while without talking. Any second now, I know I'm going to get restless from being stuck in one place for so long, and extra restless from the quiet. But it's nice for a while. It's nice just lying here in comfortable silence. Even after all our ups and downs this week, I'm glad I've got my siblings.

"Hey, can I ask a hypothetical question?" I say before I can lose my nerve.

Rose perks up immediately. "I love hypothetical questions," she says.

"Hypothetically," I say, and I take a deep breath. I can hardly believe that I'm having this conversation with them, much less having it during the daytime. My chest feels warm again, though—that little glow that comes from being Simon. "Say I wanted to go by a different name? And different pronouns?"

It's scary saying it out loud. Even scarier knowing that I can see them and they can see me. But they're both starting to smile. Rose reaches over and squeezes one of my hands, and Talia reaches over to grab my other one. They take each other's hands, too. Finishing the circle.

"Hypothetically," Talia says, "I would say okay. I'd say that's awesome, and I'm glad you're figuring out who you are."

"I'd be excited for you," Rose says.

"And proud of you," Talia says.

"Hypothetically," Rose adds.

That glowing feeling is spreading through me all the way now. All the way to my fingertips and then spilling over.

"Cool," I say. "Cool." I can feel myself smiling, and it's not forced or conscious this time. I'm just smiling because I'm happy. Because I'm okay. I hadn't realized until this moment how heavy it had been sitting on me. This question of what they would say. How they would react. I'd been telling myself it was fine, telling myself I wasn't really worried. But the relief and excitement I'm feeling now hits me in a wave.

I must've been worried without letting myself realize it, because now that I'm *not* worried, I'm practically giddy.

I take another deep breath. "So I want to go by a different name," I say. "I mean, I've already been going by it in my head. I think I want to start having other people call me by it, too."

And I tell them.

✳✳✳

Even though our little under-the-bed gathering isn't officially a Sibling Conference, we still agree on an action item from it.

"So," Talia says, "new name and pronouns for Simon." And she actually says "Simon." I don't have to fix it in my head. She keeps saying it out loud, like she knows that every time she does, it makes the glowing feeling in me glow even brighter. I didn't think I had space in me for any more happy, but somehow it's still growing. "And keep us updated if *he* and *him* stops feeling right, okay?" Talia adds. "Or if something else feels *more* right."

"Will do," I say. I can't stop smiling. It's not an on-purpose smile, just a happy one—like the one Brie had in that photo of her and the girl at that bake sale. The kind of smile you do for yourself and not a camera.

"Are you going to tell Mom and Dad?" Rose asks me. "And Nanaleen?"

"Yeah," I say. "Soon, at least. Can..." I swallow and start again. "Can you both be there when I do?"

Rose and Talia both agree right away. Of course they do.

So that's the action item from our unofficial Sibling Conference. We don't even have to vote on it officially. It's already unanimous. As we all crawl out from under the bed, all three of us kicking and laughing and elbowing each other in the face, I realize suddenly that Simon isn't my secret name anymore.

Now it's just my name.

Family Meal

MOM AND DAD DRIVE DOWN IN TIME FOR LUNCH. I HELP NANALEEN cook breakfast-for-lunch, and she has us set the table with "the good place settings," which means the plates that aren't chipped and also one of her nice white tablecloths from the linen cabinet. I have to bring down the bag from our failed séance last night and return Nanaleen's good candles to her. And I apologize to her for breaking her bowl.

"We could maybe still glue it back," I offer when I show her the broken pieces.

Nanaleen just shakes her head, though. She doesn't look mad or even sad about the broken dish. "That's all right," she says. "It's had a good run. Sometimes you have to know when to let things go."

When Mom and Dad's car pulls up to the top of the driveway, we all meet them out on the porch. Dad goes down the line kissing each of us on the forehead, just like he did when he was dropping us off. Mom squeezes each of us into a hug.

"Hey, kiddo," she says as she's hugging me. "Missed you this week."

"Missed you, too," I tell her.

"What's that amazing smell?" Dad says, leaning through the open doorway into the front hall. The house doesn't *not* smell musty and sour, the way it has all week. But right now there's the smell of sausage and eggs and biscuits with gravy all spread over the top of it, and we all know that's the part Dad's pointing out.

Nanaleen's not done cooking yet, though, and when I try to help her, she shoos me back into the living room.

"Go entertain your folks," she tells me. And I have a feeling she knows we all have some things to talk about.

In the living room, Mom and Dad and Rose are all crammed onto the sofa, and Talia has taken

Nanaleen's recliner. The old black-and-white family photos are smiling down at them, just as happy and perfect as always. Although with everything we've been trying to figure out about Brie, I'm starting to realize that photos framed on the wall or lined up neatly in an album aren't telling the full story.

Not even close.

I think about trying to fit myself onto the couch with all of them, but instead I settle into another chair so I can see everyone's faces. They've already been talking. For the first few seconds I worry that I've been missing part of an important conversation, but I haven't, because they're all talking about nothing again.

"How was your week?" Talia is asking.

"Not bad," Dad says right away, easy-breezy.

"Pretty quiet," Mom says. "Pretty uneventful."

"It rained a couple times," Dad says. "Did it rain more here?"

"Yeah, sure," Talia says. And then she says, "Did you have time to . . . *talk*?"

She puts weight on it, and Mom and Dad look at each other for a couple seconds, like they're having a silent conversation. Their easy-breezy smiles fade for just a moment before Dad manages to pull his back on.

"Sure," Dad says. "We talked some. We were pretty busy pining after you, though." He gives me a wink. I don't wink back.

"You can talk to us about stuff, you know," I say.

Everybody's quiet for a long, long while. Nanaleen is still in the next room, but I even hear her scraping of the spatula go quiet for a second. The quiet goes on for so long that it eats at my edges, but Rose chimes in before I have to push on.

"Yeah," Rose says. "Like, you don't have to tell us *everything*. But we all know something's going on."

Talia looks to both of us. "We all wish you'd tell us the actual story, so we don't end up making up one on our own."

Mom and Dad are having a silent conversation with their eyes. Even though I agree with everything Talia and Rose have said, every instinct in me is telling me to make it stop. To say something lighthearted and distracting to smooth this over. To divert the conversation to something easier. Mom and Dad look uncomfortable, and I *feel* uncomfortable, and all my instincts are to fix it.

You're allowed to have feelings, you know. You don't have to be happy all the time.

And so I don't jump in. I don't try to make the conversation light or easy-breezy.

I just listen.

And then they finally talk to us.

The way Dad describes it, they've been stressed for a long while because of Dad losing his job and struggling to find a new one, and worrying about having enough money in the meantime. And then the stress from all these big things keeps spilling over into stress over lots of little things, too, and instead of finding good outlets and working through it all together, they've been taking it out on each other.

I can relate to that a little too well.

The way Mom describes it, it's all those things, all those stresses, and it's also this: Both of them feeling kind of stuck. Feeling like they're a little bit lost, a little bit unsure of who they are and how they fit together anymore.

"We met when we were so young," Mom says. "But the people we've grown into aren't the same people we were when we were eighteen."

"Which is a good thing!" Dad cuts in.

"Which is a good thing," Mom agrees. "But it also means we have to sort of...see how we work now." She meets Dad's eyes again and they have one more silent conversation. "Or *if* we work at all."

They don't know exactly what they're going to do from here, they tell us. They've started counseling, and they're figuring out what'll be best for us all—for the short term *and* the long term. For them *and* for us kids. In my mind, I can imagine two different futures for us all: One where Mom and Dad stay together, where we're all a family under one roof. Or one where they don't. And our family changes. And we all have to learn a new version of it.

I'm thinking about the index cards in the backs of the old children's books at the library here— the ones that only knew the version of Mom as a kid. And I'm thinking about Mom's old high school yearbook, and the photo of her that looked so much younger than she is now, but also almost just the same. Nanaleen's described Mom and Dad's romance as a perfect love story, but nobody's is, I guess. That short version of the story doesn't tell the whole thing. It's like the old family photos.

I look up at the empty spot where the photo I borrowed for our séance is supposed to be. And I look at the one beside it—the first photo without Brie. There isn't a shadowy figure in the background of it—just regular shadows. But I understand why my brain imagined it there the other day.

The photo feels like it's missing something.

"Can we talk about Nanaleen and the house?" I ask finally.

Nanaleen comes in from the kitchen for this part, and she doesn't seem at all surprised by what we're talking about. I can tell that this is all part of a bigger conversation she and Mom and Dad have been having for a while already. Because Nanaleen wants to stay here, in her home, but she also wants to be with her family, and her home needs more care and attention than it's been getting for a while, and there isn't an easy answer. Mom talks about some of the ideas she and Aunt Shannon and Aunt Bridget have had. Aunt Bridget could come to stay with Nanaleen for a while. Nanaleen could move in with us in Louisville. There's a lot of different ways the family could try to move around. There are too many possible futures for me to imagine here—too many things that might happen in different ways.

As they talk, though, I'm thinking about making dough with Nanaleen. About the windowpane test she always does, holding up the dough and stretching it thin to check if you can see the light through it. We're still in the messy stage of dough-making right now—still in the part when we've only just mixed the ingredients, but we haven't kneaded them all together yet. We haven't gotten it smooth and elastic. Right now, everything is still sticky and confusing, and it's hard to even really believe that it's all going to come together to form something in the end. It's hard to even know how it's going to look.

But I decide that I can trust that it *will* come together. Eventually. Somehow. It's a lot easier to trust that when we're all actually acknowledging that it's happening. When we're all actually talking about it.

We talk until way past when we'd planned to eat lunch, but Nanaleen has left all the ingredients out in the kitchen, and we all pitch in to help finish up the cooking. I'm stirring gravy, and Dad is scrambling the eggs, and Talia and Rose finish cooking the sausages while Mom gets the table set.

I accidentally spill a bunch of gravy on the floor, though, and half the sausages come out burned, and by the time we get all of it onto the table, the kitchen is a mess. We're all a little bit of a mess, too. When we sit down to eat, Dad has eggs stuck to one of his sleeves, and I've got a smear of gravy on my front that I don't even remember when it got there.

It's not a picture-perfect family meal or anything. None of it's perfect. It's just us.

There's a question that's still poking at me, one I've been wondering about all week but have been afraid to ask, because I don't know if I'm going to like the answer. But I guess I'd rather get the real answer than just the one I've been making up in my mind.

I pass Nanaleen the bowl of biscuits, and then I say, "Can I ask you something about your sister Brie?"

Mom's eyes get big. "Brie?"

"It's okay if you say no," I tell Nanaleen quickly, but Nanaleen is smiling. She takes the biscuits from me, and then she pats my hand.

"Ask away," she says.

And so finally, I get to ask Nanaleen why Brie left.

Nanaleen's face is sad. At first, I want to cheer her up, but I don't—she's sad because this is a sad thing. "Our parents drove her away," Nanaleen says.

She pauses for a long while after that, like she's deciding how much she wants to say. When she goes on, though, her face is resolved.

"She fell in love with a girl," Nanaleen says. Beside me, I feel Talia lean forward a little in her seat. I only give myself a second to glance at her, but her eyes are wide, hanging on Nanaleen's every word. "When she told our parents that she was a lesbian, they didn't take it well."

She frowns at her own words.

"No, that's an understatement," she corrects. "They were right awful about it. They wanted to make her change. But she wasn't having it. She left. I was devastated that she left at the time, but now, I know it was for the best." Nanaleen's a little misty-eyed by now. "And after she was gone, our parents just didn't talk about her. They didn't talk about what had happened. I was so young when she went, and I didn't even know the full story for a long time. But we all let it go on for much too long."

Mom and Dad aren't the only ones in our family who've avoided talking about hard things, I guess.

Mom's looking a little misty-eyed, too. She leans into Nanaleen's side, and then she studies me across the table. "Where's this coming from, anyway?" Mom asks.

"We were doing a little family history this week," I say, and Rose and Talia and I tell them about the yearbooks at the Misty Valley Public Library.

Nanaleen's grinning ear to ear by the time we're finished. "I didn't know you all were so interested in family history," she says.

"I didn't, either!" I laugh. But it turns out I like getting the real stories behind some of the old photos. Even when we're *not* trying to investigate ghosts.

My brain's jumping all around, just like it usually is, but I don't try so hard to hang on to it right now. I'm thinking about the look on Talia's face when Nanaleen had said that Brie fell in love with a girl. I'm thinking about my secret name—and about how it's not totally a secret anymore. I'm thinking about that first Sunday school class when Mrs. Evans told us the meaning of St. Peter's new name, and about looking up the meaning of Simon after class, too. *Listen.*

I'm thinking about all the ways I can keep growing into my name.

"I think I'd really like hearing more of the family stories," I tell Nanaleen now. "And hearing more about your sister. Maybe next time we visit, or . . . ?" I don't know what our next visit will look like or where it'll be, and Nanaleen doesn't, either. But she pats my cheek and nods.

"I think I'd like sharing them with you," she says.

Going Home

I'M PACKING UP MY BACKPACK IN THE DORMITORY WHEN I remember the jacket.

Nanaleen is down on the front porch watching Mom and Dad load up our car. When I come down to find her, she recognizes the bundle of leather in my arms before I even hold it up.

"That was Brie's," she says. She lets me push the jacket into her hands, and she holds it close to her, smiling at it a little fondly like it's not just a jacket—it's her sister Brianna right here with us.

"I found it in the closet upstairs," I say, and then I add, "and I found this in the pocket."

I pull out the note that had been folded inside

the jacket—the one signed from Jo with a heart. Nanaleen reads it, and then she reads it again. She has a faraway look on her face.

"Jo," she says. "I remember Jo. She was Brie's..." She pauses for a long moment, and then she smiles. "Her girlfriend," she tells me. "They told everybody they were friends, but Brie told me years later Jo was her girlfriend."

I make a note to tell Talia that my guess had been right about that, too. But then I replay Nanaleen's words in my head. "Wait. Years later? Did you get to talk to her again after she left?"

"As a matter of fact, I did," Nanaleen says. "Much, much later, but we got to reconnect before she passed. We had so much to catch up on. She was happy, though. She made a family for herself out there in California, and she made a good life for herself." Nanaleen is quiet for a minute, thinking, and then she beams. "I even got to go to her wedding."

I must be gaping at her. "Her *wedding*?"

Nanaleen's nodding. "Mm-hmm. You were pretty

little, and Rose wasn't even born yet, I guess. But she and her wife had been together for almost fifty years before they tied the knot. I got to fly out there when they made it official."

I'm grinning from ear to ear by now. Not a forced smile—this is the kind of smile that's so big you can't help it. There's a warm, glowing feeling inside my chest, filling me all the way up.

"I've got the pictures somewhere up in the history room," she says. "I haven't gotten them into albums yet, but maybe I should do those next."

"Definitely," I say. "Talia and I can help you next time we're here." I don't feel bad volunteering Talia to help with sorting the photos. I have a feeling she'll be happy to be a part of it.

Nanaleen hands the jacket back to me.

"Right," I say. "I'll go put this back where I got it."

But when I start for the door, Nanaleen stops me. "Weren't we going to find you a jacket that fits this week? This one looks about your size."

I stare at her. "I can't take this."

"Why not?"

"I don't want to ruin it," I say, even though I don't want to give it back yet. "It's really old, right? What if I—I don't know—spill something on it?"

Nanaleen raises an eyebrow at me. "It'll wash, won't it? What, do you not have washing machines in the city?"

That makes me laugh. "But what if it gets worn out?" I ask.

Nanaleen shrugs. "I'd rather it get used and worn out than just sit here in the closet forever. Wouldn't you?"

The jacket is a little big still, but I'll have room to grow into it. I like to think that, if my great-aunt Brie were still alive, she'd be happy I'm taking it.

Mom and Dad are almost finished loading the car, so I rush back inside and up to the Dormitory to grab my backpack and make sure I haven't forgotten anything. I probably still will, but we'll be back. From all the way down on the porch, I can hear Nanaleen talking to our parents.

Footsteps come thundering up the Dormitory stairs, and then Talia's head appears.

"Come on, Simon," she says, gesturing down the stairs. "Time to go."

And she really says "Simon." She says it like it's the easiest thing in the world. I feel that warm glow starting in my chest, filling me up, spreading to my fingertips. I let it spill out of me.

I grin and follow her out of the house.

Acknowledgments

First, a huge thank-you to my editor, Nikki Garcia, and editorial assistant Milena Blue Spruce for guiding me through every step of this whirlwind process. You were able to sort through my tangled, scattered mess of a first draft and gently point out what I'd unknowingly written the book about, and I can't thank you both enough for helping this story become what it is. Your brilliant questions and observations make the book so much stronger every time.

I'm incredibly grateful for the amazing team at Little, Brown Books for Young Readers and the hard work you all do to get books out into the world and help them shine. Thank you to art director Karina Granda and designer Gabrielle Chang for this book's design, and thank you to Celia Krampien for bringing Simon to life so beautifully in your cover art. Thank you to production editor Marisa Finkelstein, copy editor Daniel Lupo, proofreaders Sarah Vostok and Ariana dos Santos, production and manufacturing coordinator Patricia Alvarado, marketer Bill Grace and assistant marketer Andie Divelbiss, digital marketer Mara Brashem, school and library marketer Christie Michel, publicist Cheryl Lew, and everyone at Little, Brown Books for Young Readers.

Thank you, Beth Phelan, phenomenal agent and phenomenal person, for everything you do and for helping me coax a scrap of an idea into this story that I'm so proud of. I'm so grateful to have you by my side.

Thank you so much to all the fellow writers I've connected with online and the virtual writing groups that have been getting me through the ups and downs of this process. Thank you a thousand times to my amazing Lambda family and the Flamin Blazin chat: Kirt Ethridge, Jas Hammonds, Caitlin Hernandez, Sacha Lamb, Avery Mead, Octavia Saenz, JD Scott, and Jen St. Jude. I'm not exaggerating when I say I wouldn't have made it to this point of my writing journey without you, and I'm so grateful to have you all in my life.

Thank you to Natalie Morgan and Katherine Ouellette for the countless evenings of drafting, brainstorming, commiserating, and encouraging one another. You make writing so much less lonely and are the best friends I could ask for.

Thank you, Mom, Dad, Mom Tom, and Grandad, for all your love and support over the years and for cheering me on along this journey. And thank you to my amazing, goofy, weird, wonderful siblings, Megan, Kate, Kevin, and Tricia: You're the reason I love sibling stories so much.

Finally, thank you to my wife, Cara, for helping me work through all my plot problems, gently talking me down when I'm stressed, giving me affirmation when I need it, keeping the house together when I'm on deadline, and for always reminding me about what matters. I love you.